The route Longarm was following seemed just about right for a mountain goat.

At last he crawled around a pile of house-sized boulders to see a light in a window ahead. He stared soberly at the small, bright square. Had it not been so nasty out, he'd have considered waiting till sunrise to make his play. But he doubted it was midnight yet, and he knew that at this altitude he was already dangerously chilled.

He decided, *what the hell*, and advanced with his gun trained on the one door in or out. If he could kick it in with his first try, he'd have a good chance of getting the drop on them. Should the damn door hold, he'd be in a whole lot of trouble.

He made up his mind to kick like hell...

TABOR EVANS

ON DEATH MOUNTAIN

A JOVE BOOK

LONGARM ON DEATH MOUNTAIN

A Jove Book/published by arrangement with
the author

PRINTING HISTORY
Jove edition/April 1987

ISBN: 0-515-08934-6

Jove Books are published by the Berkley Publishing Group,
200 Madison Avenue, New York, NY 10016.
The words "A JOVE BOOK" and the "J" with sunburst
are trademarks belonging to Jove Publications, Inc.

PRINTED IN THE UNITED STATES OF AMERICA

Chapter 1

Nobody could get to work at the Denver Federal Building earlier than U.S. Marshal Vail. He had the key to the office. But Longarm was waiting for his boss on the dawn-wet granite steps with a sheepish smile and empty pockets, hoping to find Billy in a good mood, or at least not as mad as he usually was after opening the morning mail.

But no man who expected his wife to cook breakfast for him before rooster-crow could expect to get down to the job with his stomach feeling anything but pain and, as he correctly surmised what his senior deputy was doing up so early, Billy Vail growled, "The answer is no. The taxpayers of these United States pay you better than five hundred a year to keep them safe from harm. You're supposed to manage your money betwixt paydays, not blow it all on wine, women, and them awful cheroots you smoke. I told you the last time it was the last time I'd give you an advance before the middle of the month, you carefree heathen!"

As Vail unlocked the big bronze doors Longarm pro-

1

tested, "It ain't the middle of the month, Billy. I paid heed to your advice and this month I managed to make my modest money last till *less'n* two weeks before payday!"

Vail opened the door. "No, no, a thousand times no, like the gal in that song says," he growled.

Longarm persisted, "Hell, she was strapped down in a sawmill by a villain, Billy. You know I ain't after your maidenly virtue. I only want you to advance me some eating money. How would it look if a deputy U.S. marshal had to beg for his bread on Larimer Street?"

Vail smiled despite himself. "It might teach you a good lesson. I swear *I've* never been able to get through to you. I told you Friday I'd heard about the Sunday-Go-To-Meeting-On-The-Green that First Methodist was giving. I told you just how dangerous them cake sales could get when the gal who'd baked the cake was worth bidding up. But did you listen? Hell, no, you *never* listen, and it serves you right if the pretty gal who no doubt baked an ugly cake never even let you kiss her, after."

"Things didn't get quite that bad, Billy," Longarm said. "But there was this one fool cowhand bidding against me for her cake and considerable good graces and, I swear, he must have wanted her prune-whip topping even more than I did."

As they clomped along the deserted marble halls Vail asked, "How come you let him bid you up so high, then?" Longarm's sorrow seemed sincere when he explained, "I didn't know how flat her pastry might be, until she let me at it, later."

2

Vail laughed like hell. But as they climbed the marble stairwell together he said, "Variety can be the spice of life or, just as often, not worth the trouble. That's why I been married-up with the same woman so long, old son. If you had a lick of sense you'd find someone special and marry up with her."

Longarm grimaced. "If I had a lick of sense I wouldn't be working for such a cheap outfit. A top hand makes as much as I do, since the price of beef's been up, and he hardly ever gets shot, either."

Vail unlocked the door to their office and snorted, "You had your chance to shoot it out with cows in your misspent youth just after the War. You know you like packing a badge, Longarm. Where else could you get a job that lets you fight so much with a good excuse?"

Longarm followed him in, complaining, "I don't mind the fringe benefits and I don't mind the hours. But the pay is ridiculous."

The older lawman bent to pick up the letters and wires that had been shoved through the door slot. Then he led the way into his back office. He tossed the new communications on his battered desk and took time to adjust the banjo clock on the oak-paneled wall at least two hairs, forward, of course.

Then he hung up his hat, sat down at his desk, and began to open his mail. Longarm unbuttoned his tweed frock coat, exposing the worn grips of his cross-draw .44-40, and took a seat in the leather guest chair facing the desk. He tried to say something. Vail snapped, "Don't pester me when I'm busy, damn it." So Longarm took a three-for-a-nickel cheroot from his vest pocket and lit up. Vail tried to ignore him, but the second time he flicked ash on the rug Vail snapped, "Cut that out. If I've told you once I've told you a hundred times I don't have carpet beetles and, even if I did, I'd let the little bastards get their own tobacco."

"Did I have two dimes to rub together I could wait over to the Parthenon Saloon while you got more organized this blue Monday morning, Billy," Longarm observed.

Vail said, "Don't want you drinking needled beer. I find your unusual devotion to duty this morning a pleasant novelty. So just set, try not to set my rug on fire, and I may find something for you to do. I see we got a hired gun going to trial down the hall any minute now. The judge feels it would look more seemly if we had him covered polite instead of making him take the stand in leg irons. How do you feel about a quiet morning in court, old son?"

Longarm said, "Awful. This is my next to last smoke and I read the yellow sheets on that case. The bastard ain't got a chance, but he's got a good lawyer, and it could take days to find him hangable. That's a poor chore to offer a deputy with my seniority, Billy."

Vail didn't answer. He was grinning from ear to ear as he read a long Western Union night letter from Jamestown, Colorado. He couldn't wait until he got to the bottom line. "It's no wonder you're always broke, Longarm. How much did you have to pay for that mountain of yours up in Grand County, anyways?"

Longarm had been teased about that before. He'd never thought it was all that funny. He said, "If my name was Vail I'd have a mine named after me. Long's Peak was discovered way back in 1816 by an army survey team led by one Colonel Stephen H. Long. No relation to me as far as I can tell. You can say it's in Grand County or you can say it's in Boulder County. It ain't for me to say. It's also a good ten miles from Jimtown by crow, and a good day's ride on anything else, since trails run crooked as hell up in the front range. So why is Jimtown worried about Long's Peak? Have they lost it?"

Vail read on. "Not hardly, but they just lost the considerable contents of the post office safe up there, so it's federal. This yell for help would have been sent Friday afternoon, since it was sent night-letter rates by some cheap bastard to be delivered Saturday morning. I'm reading it this late in the game because me and Henry left early on Saturday. To sign for that hired gun at the depot, not to buy cakes, by the way."

Longarm grimaced and said, "This is no time to bring up past mistakes about pastry, boss. I was with you up to the Jimtown post office safe. How in thunder did Long's Peak get into all this?"

"It wasn't a safe cracking. It was stand-up robbery at two in the afternoon, when most of the men in town were working in the mine and there was nobody to do much more than scream as they rode out, blowing away one of the few streetlamps in town as well as a town deputy who tried to stop them solo. He wasn't one of our own, exactly, but he was law, and he was gunned by rascals committing a federal crime. So I'm calling it murder-one under federal jurisdiction, in addition to the federal crime of sticking up a post office and scaring federal employees half to death."

Longarm smiled a wolfish hunting smile and said, "I like it when a case is so uncomplicated. How many murderous owlhoots are we talking about?"

"This wire doesn't say. Just mentions a mighty noisy gang. No descriptions at all. They must have been still sort of rattled by the ride-out when they sent this. By the time you get there a lot of townies will no doubt recall more details, whether they saw them or not."

"I've noticed that in the past," Longarm said. "But I sure wish you'd tell me how a mountain miles away fits in to that Jimtown robbery."

Vail said, "The gang lit out west along the mountain wagon trace between Jamestown and Ward. Same county. Same sheriff's posse."

"I know that road. It has hairpins all over the place," Longarm said.

Vail said, "The posse knew that as well. They wired ahead up to Ward. The deputies and half the miners in Ward formed a head-off, a broad-faced one, only the gang never rid into 'em."

Longarm thought and decided, "I can think of more'n one place a bashful gent aboard a pony could get to, off that wagon trace. It's rough country but it's cow country. All sorts of bitty valley parks running every which way. Plenty of tall timber as well. Aspen ain't worth shit as lumber, but it sure grows thick and tall enough. Get to the part about Long's Peak. I can think of many a place to hole up between Ward and Jimtown, and all of 'em make more sense than mountain climbing."

Vail said, "Men who work more regular up that way know the country, too. Having plenty of manpower as well as savvy, they got right to work on where the bandits might have left the main route. So they cut their trail, up along a whitewater creek running down off the heights of your very own peak, and then they followed it, higher and higher, till they lost it on the frost-shattered gravel above timberline. As you once noted in an official report about another case so far up along the divide, one can see one hell of a ways above timberline."

"That's true. But leave us never forget the alpine scenery up there is cut up considerable by gullies and such. My namesake, Colonel Long, may have *named* that part of the front range, but it's yet to be *mapped* entire by anyone."

Vail said, "The posse was made up of men who didn't need maps. They moseyed on up the slopes till they got near an old stone house where the climb commences to get serious and there's only one trail. Then somebody opened fire on 'em from the house and they had to fall back and reconsider."

Longarm looked incredulous and asked, "Billy, do you really mean to send me all the infernal way up there if the fool posse already has the gang pinned down?"

Vail growled, "I get pure tired, talking to a man who never listens," and handed Longarm the long telegraph message.

7

Longarm found nothing he didn't already know until he got to:

VOLUNTEERS GOING IN TWO HOURS LATER FOUND CABIN DESERTED STOP BLOOD AND EMPTY BEAN CANS BY FIRE-PLACE STOP ASSUME SUSPECTS MOVE ON UP STOP PEAK FOURTEEN THOUSAND FEET HIGH AND TREACHEROUS THIS TIME OF YEAR STOP WE ARE NOT MOUNTAIN GOATS AND IF WE WERE THERE ARE AT LEAST A DOZEN OF THEM UP THERE STOP DO YOU HAVE ANYONE WILLING TO SCALE MOUNTAIN UNDER FIRE QUESTION MARK DEPUTY JUNG BOULDER SHERIFFS DEPARTMENT.

Longarm handed the message back. "Do I look like a fool mountain goat to you?" he asked.

"What say you get up there and see what you can do, old son?" Vail asked.

Longarm said, "Damn it, Billy, that posse has the rascals treed. They're already making all the smart moves. It would be dumb as hell to go up the mountain after them. I don't meant to brag on my mountain, but she's a real bitch of busted-up up rock and snowfields a gent would have enough trouble with when nobody was tossing boulders and bullets down on him. It makes a lot more sense to just wait the gang out now that it's backed its fool self into a sort of eagle's cage. How long could anyone expect to hold out up there?"

Vail said, "Too long to hold a posse big enough to surround a mountain together. You know as well as I do that half the riders have already lost their first enthusiasm by now. Any fool kid is willing to join a posse. It takes a man to stick with one as the novelty wears off and the discomfort and tedium sets in. A man up among snowfields ain't about to get thirsty enough to surrender to the hangman. Lord knows how much grub they have with 'em and, in a pinch, a man could figure a diet of wild onion and marmot or even bird has to taste better than one's last meal in a prison cell."

"They'll freeze to death if they stay up there past October at the latest, Billy."

"Don't care about October. This is August and I want 'em *now*. I'll tell you what, you'll need some expense money as you go after them mountainous rascals. So maybe I can advance you some after all."

"Oh, well, since you put it that way, consider the poor bastards caught," Longarm said.

Chapter 2

Long's Peak was less well known than Pikes Peak to the south, not because it wasn't as high—it was actually higher—but because the human mind was better at grasping simple points.

Whereas Pikes Peak simply shot up as an exclamation point on the front range, standing alone as a majestic white cone, the taller Long's Peak had the company of little brothers and sisters that were mighty mountains in their own right, and one had to be some distance away to notice the crest of Long's Peak was up there alone in the Colorado sky when one studied on it. Rooted in higher country than Pikes Peak to begin with, just where the lower slopes of the Long's Peak massif started climbing was more a state of mind than contour lines on any survey map. The jagged summit—one had several big bumps to choose from once one got there— was for sure in Boulder County. The slopes to the north rose from Grand or Larimer Counties, sort of, as all the trails up bumped up and down over complicated geology. While each dip bottomed out a little higher in elevation than the last, it could sure feel like one was riding downhill a lot on the way up to where the peak got to rising seriously.

Surrounding so much confusion would have been a lot more confusion had not the local law called on Uncle Sam for help. While Longarm had been packing, Billy Vail had been sending wires. So by the time Longarm rode into Jimtown, near sunset, he wasn't surprised to see an army guidon fluttering near the Stars and Stripes of the shot-up post office. During less interesting times the post office there was as much or more a general store, with the business of selling stamps and reading other folks' postcards relegated to perhaps a fifth of the frame building in the back. Longarm's notes said the old lady who usually sold calico and soda crackers out front was the appointed postmistress and she in turn put her help to sorting mail and such when they had nothing more important to do out front. Naturally, the part-time postal employees still qualified as federal employees and hence were under federal protection whenever they were not cutting yard goods or sweeping up around the cracker barrel.

As Longarm dismounted out front and tethered the army mount he had picked up in Lyons from the South Saint Vrain Remount Station, a familiar figure in faded army blue came out to greet him. Longarm and Captain Matt Kincaid had ridden together in the past, mostly against Cheyenne, and had learned to trust one another in a pinch.

Kincaid said, "We've been expecting you, Longarm. Quite some time, as a matter of fact. I suppose you know you'll freeze your ass up here after dark in that sissy tweed suit?"

Longarm shook hands and explained, "Got me a sheepskin coat, a rain slicker, and some climbing jeans in my bedroll, Matt. I got here when I got here for two reasons. In the first place you can't get here, sensible. I took the train to Lyons, which is as close as civilization comes to these parts. As I was borrowing that gelding the remount sergeant explained the reasons I had to settle for such a miserable specimen of crowbait. Once I knew the army was pitching in to surround the mountain I gave up trying to get here sudden on a mighty slow mount. The twisty twenty-odd miles from Lyons to here are sort of scenic." He shot a disgusted glance at the old chestnut. "I saw more of it, for longer, than I really wanted to. I don't suppose you'd have a decent spare I could use while I'm up here?"

The captain, overage in grade but about Longarm's age and fitness, said, "Not here. I've got my dragoons spread from here to hell and breakfast. We're using the scene of the crime, here, as our command post. You won't want to ride any farther tonight, in any case. The slopes around the peak will be shrouded in considerable darkness before even a decent horse could get you there, and my boys have the rascals pinned down—or maybe *up* would be a more accurate way to put it."

Longarm fished out two cheroots as he mused, "I dunno, Matt. Seems to me that if I was boxed up a mountain I'd consider the hours of darkness the best time to bust out."

He held out a cheroot to Kincaid, who shook his

head. "No thanks, I prefer tobacco, not those mysterious whatevers you seem so fond of. There's a full moon rising bright tonight over wide-open alpine meadowland."

"I read the almanac coming up on the train from Denver. We're still discussing one hell of a circle, Matt. No offense, but if you got enough troops to surround that much ground, continuous, you ought to have at least one star instead of railroad tracks on your shoulders about now."

Kincaid grimaced. "Tell the War Department that. I've got just under two hundred dragoons to work with, and you're right, they're spread sort of thin. But they're not alone. We have posse riders from three counties around the mountain now. It's not as long a line as it might look on the map. There's a lot of slope we don't have to cover. Much of the treacherous scree we do have covered would make for mighty careful riding in broad daylight. If those outlaws mean to bust through us, they'll have a hard, noisy chore indeed. If we don't get them, the mountain will. The trails the map says are *safe* look sort of spooky in places."

Longarm glanced northward at the darkening sky. He knew the peak under discussion was perhaps a ten-mile crow-flap from where they were jawing about it. He couldn't see it. You had to stand back farther to see the front range. Once you were this far up into it the surrounding skyline looked more like treetops and the rounded granite of lesser but closer topography. He said, "Well, I meant to start by scouting sign around that cabin where the bandits were last spotted. But reading sign in the dark can be a chore. So, as long as I'm here, I may as well ask questions."

They clomped up the wooden steps and went inside. Someone had already lit the oil lamp hanging over the grocery counter. Matt Kincaid's company clerk, a lance corporal who reminded Longarm of Henry from his own office in army blue, had set up a folding desk between the cracker barrel and the unlit pot-bellied stove. The boy didn't look old enough to drink, so the bottle on the desk had to be the captain's.

But Kincaid wasn't offering him a drink. He was introducing Longarm to Mrs. Polly Clark, the postmistress, who was behind her counter in a polka-dot cotton mother hubbard. After that the notes Billy Vail had offered Longarm back in Denver were all out of joint.

As the pretty little redhead dimpled at him, Longarm reconsidered his notes and decided they weren't as wrong as they were presupposing. On second glance the widow woman who'd inherited her position from her late husband could be over thirty, as recorded. Billy Vail had never said to expect an old lady. He had just said the postmistress treated so rudely by the outlaws seemed to be a widow woman called Aunt Polly by the Jimtown miners and cowhands off the surrounding spreads. Since old Billy came with a naturally suspicious nature, he'd spent more time on the wire checking out the background of the lady who had been entrusted with considerable cash she no longer had in her possession. Both the post office and the First Bank of Boulder had given her a clean bill of health as a lady they'd known some time. Neither had reported she was pretty as a picture.

Longarm found it easy to smile back at her as he said he was sure sorry she'd been held up and asked if she had any further light to shed on the subject.

She moved down the counter, saying, "I'll show you around in the back. You have to sort of roll over this counter, though. There's no doorway on your side."

Longarm did. So did Kincaid, as she unlocked the narrow door at the end of the counter, struck a match, and stepped inside the narrow space running between the back wall and the partition between the postal operation and the rest of her retail business.

As she lit an oil lamp on the postal counter, Longarm saw that it stood near the brass-barred little window one shoved mail or stamps through, depending. The back wall was lined half with private post office boxes and half with wooden sorting slots. The far end was occupied by a fair-sized Mosler safe, its heavy door now gaping and its interior looking mighty forlorn.

Polly Clark pointed at it. "You can see how they cleaned us out," she said ruefully. "It was all so fast, as I told the law before, I barely got a look at them before they were in and out and gone. I was sorting mail with my back to the window and the next thing I knew I was on the floor, so—"

"Sitting on what?" Longarm cut in, explaining, "I don't see no chair in here, ma'am."

Kincaid said, "I can explain that. My clerk out front is sitting on it. Since Miss Polly closed the post office until further notice, we took the liberty."

Before Longarm could answer, the attractive postmistress said, "I wasn't sitting in it. I was standing right here, sorting the incoming mail. The bentwood chair was yonder, near the cage. It had nothing to do with the robbery. As I said, it was just a zim-zam, thank you ma'am, and they were running out, laughing, by the time I sat up to surmise something mighty odd had just taken place."

Longarm looked back at the narrow way they had all just come in through. "Was that door unlocked or did they bust in?" he asked.

She sighed. "I wish you hadn't asked that. I surely *mean* to keep it locked from now on, but as one has to climb over the counter to get to it, and as I'm usually running back and forth between selling stamps and provisions—"

Longarm shushed her with an understanding smile and said, "Let's talk about the safe. How come they found that open as well?"

She looked insulted. "They didn't. I'd locked it about an hour before. I remember the time because I'd just had to sign a receipt for the money bags those rascals carried off with them, maybe not over my dead body, but certainly my body as I lay there stunned."

Longarm already had the amount and the names of the miners who figured to get paid late in his notebook. He asked her, "Where were the two postal clerks reported as was pistol-whipped while all this was going on, ma'am?"

"Out front," she said, "actually putting a new shipment of stock on the shelves. The gang came in, simply knocked everybody out of the way, and the rest you know."

17

She saw he was still staring at the open safe. "I know what you're thinking," she went on. "Deputy Jung asked me about that when he was first on the scene. Neither of my clerks opened up for the robbers. I didn't either. They opened it themselves, helped themselves to the money, and just scooted."

Being army instead of law, it was Kincaid who suggested, "They must have known the combination. They knew when to hit, as well."

Longarm shot him a disgusted look and said, "Matt, the first thing I like to say about a possible inside job is nothing much."

"I've already had that out with Deputy Jung," Polly Clark snapped. "Neither of the gents I hire as part-time help when I have the work for them knows the combination to that safe. They were out front, in no position to help those awful men, and it's not fair to pick on two poor pistol-whipped boys like that! I was back here alone. I *do* know the combination. If you have to suspect someone working here, I suggest you start by suspecting me, damn it!"

Longarm nodded pleasantly. "I already do, ma'am, if that's any comfort to you. A suspicious nature comes with the badge I'm packing," he said.

Kincaid said, "Oh, come on, Custis. You know as well as I do we're dealing with outsiders here. Who but a stranger to these parts would trap his fool self on a mountain less than a full day's ride from here?"

"I don't know. I ain't had a chance to talk to 'em yet. Before I head over to the mountain for a word with 'em I'd best see what other victims has to say. Did that one gent they gunned have any last words on the subject that someone here in town might recall?"

The pretty postmistress said, "My boys are out with the posse, looking for the brutes, of course. Just about every able-bodied man in town is, as you might imagine. The rascals rode off with everyone's eating money for the foreseeable future. As for that poor boy they gunned, he might have said something to the first ones who got to him. They say he died before they could get him to the dentist. I didn't see it, sitting on the floor in here. By the time I heard about it he was dead and carried home to wake."

Kincaid nudged Longarm and murmured, "I can show you to the folk you want to talk to, pard. Can't you see you're upsetting the lady?"

She said she was more mad than upset. Longarm left with the army man, anyway. Outside it was really dark now. In the high country the evening stars hung down so close at night that a body felt like ducking the brighter ones. The tiny town shed little more light. But somewhere a rinky-tink piano was playing off-key and that seemed to be where Kincaid was taking Longarm.

"You don't think that poor little gal had anything to do with opening that safe, do you?" he asked.

Longarm said, "Somebody opened it. Mosler makes a good product. Her story reads two ways, assuming she's innocent at all. She could have just been careless and, not wanting the post office to give someone more careful her job here, she could be covering it up with a simple fib. Where are we headed, Matt?"

"Saloon. You said you wanted to ask about that town

19

law they gunned on the way out. I could take you up the slope to his cabin, but wakes are sort of depressing, and anyone who saw the shooting and isn't at the wake should be at the saloon. What was your second guess about that safecracking job?"

Longarm shook his head. "It wasn't cracked. It was just plain opened, whether locked or not to begin with. If she was right about how long they took getting in and out, there was no time for sneaky sandpapered fingers and an ear to the steel. Like I said, Mosler makes a pretty good safe, and while who's to say what a real old pro could do or not do in a quiet hour or so, I find it easier to believe in a gent who knew the combination to begin with."

"She just told us neither of the boys working for her had the combination, Longarm," Kincaid said.

The slightly taller deputy shrugged. "It's a bigger world than that. According to my notes, Polly Clark and her man before her have been running the Jimtown post office about three years. I'd sure like to talk to the old geezer who run it before 'em, but he's dead. So I can't ask him who he might or might not have shared such secrets with."

Kincaid nodded grimly and said, "You're good. It shouldn't be too hard to find out who might or might not have worked there before the Clarks took over, right?"

"It's always hard going back," Longarm said. "We live in changing times out here. Getting anyone to sit still three years can be a botheration. It was only three or four years ago you and me was civilizing them unreconstructed Indians, way the hell north of here, and *now* look where we are. I know a little about these parts. The population tends to be mighty transient. Mines open and close faster than a rug merchant can go in and out of business. The cattle spreads up here have trouble keeping hired help, between the uncertain price of beef and even less certain Indians."

"Hell, there hasn't been any Indian trouble up here since we rounded up Green Hand's Arapaho a couple of years ago," Kincaid said.

Longarm shrugged. "That's what I was just saying. That piano sure sounds familiar, and new to these parts as well. I'm not sure whether I hope I'm right or wrong. Things are already complicated enough for me around here tonight."

They went into the little saloon. A gal all in red was playing the upright piano with her back to the bar.

Longarm sighed and said, "Like I was saying, folk sure get around out here. Don't announce me to the crowd, Matt. I want to talk to anyone who witnessed that shooting and it's hard to get a word in edgeways once Red Robin gets up from her piano."

The army man shot an admiring glance at the statuesque woman at the piano across the room. "I might have guessed you'd know her, Longarm. I got a front view earlier today. She looks a lot better than she plays piano. Why do they call her Red Robin? Anyone can see that long black mane of hers isn't red."

"It was, the first time I met her down Texas way," Longarm said. "But I got her off the charge and since then she's let it come out natural. I don't know whether her name is Robin, Roberta, or some other name entire.

21

She's a sort of rambling rose by any name. Sometimes I get to suspecting she follows me around, for I keep running across her in the damnedest places."

Kincaid was young and healthy, too, so he asked in a desperately casual voice how serious Longarm felt about the attractive awful pianist.

"Red Robin is sort of hard to feel too serious about, Matt," Longarm said. "That's as much as a gent ought to say about a she-male fellow wanderer in this vale of tears. I won't shoot you if you want to sing along with her, if that's what you mean. I come here to talk about dead law, not lively, lawless gals."

Chapter 3

They bellied against the bar next to a skinny gent in faded denims, a Colorado-crushed black Stetson and an S&W .44 slung low, and Kincaid introduced him to Longarm as Lefty Page. Page allowed he was ramrod of the Middle Fork and they raised mostly horses and that he'd seen the killing.

He said, "I was standing near the smithy when them owlhoots tore past, Longarm. Poor old Compten was quicker thinking. So he was out in the street, slapping leather, afore I could come unstuck. I pegged a couple of parting shots after 'em as they rid over Compten and kept going. Can't say whether I hit anybody. They hit old Compten good. Riding over him didn't do much for his wounds at all. He was hit high and low and in the chest. Died before we could get him to the dentist."

Longarm nodded. "My notes say it's a choice between a dentist and a vet, here in Jimtown. Was the town law killed instant, or might he have had any comment on the gents as rode him down so surly?"

"I was the first one to reach him," Lefty said. "He

was still half-alive for mayhaps a dozen coughs. He didn't say anything sensible, though."

"What did he say, then?" Longarm asked.

Lefty replied, "Oh, you know how a gent talks after he'd been stampeded or shot. He just looked up at me, owl-eyed, and said something like 'whoever would have thought of it.' Yeah, that's exactly what he said, 'whoever would have thought it.' I asked him whoever would have thought what, but then he coughed once more, horrible, and closed his poor old eyes. Time some others come to help me pick him up, he was gone."

Longarm said, "He could have meant a lot of things. He must have been feeling surprised as well as poorly. What do you recall about the gang, Lefty?"

The ramrod frowned thoughtfully. "There were six of 'em, exactly. Two chestnuts, a roan with white stockings, a black and white paint, a buckskin with black mane and tail, and a black Morgan with a bobbed tail."

Longarm said soberly, "I was more interested in the riders than their mounts, Lefty."

The ramrod of a horse spread nodded sadly. "Deputy Jung said much the same thing, and didn't word it as polite," he said. "I know I should have paid more attention to what was aboard them six horses, but horseflesh is what I knows best. I do recall they was all dressed cow, of course."

"What about masks?" Longarm asked.

Lefty said, "Red calico bandannas. Wait, I think some of them might have slipped some. I never got a good look at any faces. But come to study on it, two in the lead was riding bare-face. They was looking Compten's way, not at me, and . . . oh, yeah, the leader wore one of them tall Texas hats. Gray, or dirty white. They didn't stick around long enough for me to study."

Longarm had a casual look around before he observed, "I don't see many other gents of the stockworking persuasion in here this evening, Lefty. I reckon most of the men fit to ride are out riding right about now, eh?"

Lefty nodded. "I offered, but I decided not to ride with the posse after Deputy Jung calt me a name I'd have had to kill him for, if I'd thought he meant it, and wasn't just upset. When he implied I was stupid as well I decided he could just hunt them owlhoots without my modest help. I've just paid my respects up to the Compten cabin and, once I fortify myself some more, I aim to go home and say good night to critters as treat me with more respect."

"The Middle Fork's halfway between here and Ward, Longarm," Kincaid explained. "We've already made sure the outlaws didn't change mounts up that way."

Lefty looked disgusted. "They never got that close to Ward. They cut up Dead Cow Creek through an aspen hell. Such a trail as there might be leads on up to Long's Peak."

Longarm raised an eyebrow and asked how anyone could learn so much, riding with red-eye rather than a posse.

Lefty explained, "I ain't the only one who don't admire the tongue-lashings of Whitey Jung. Couple of the boys rid back this way just afore you gents arrived. Slim Tracy and Spud McArtle off the Lazy W. They was so mad they could spit. But they tolt me all about their misadventures as they calmed down with a drink here, just now."

Longarm made a mental note of the names and outfit. "Did they say what might have vexed 'em so?" he asked.

Lefty said, "Sure. Deputy Jung. He's big and he's mean. But a man can only take so much mean-mouthing off a son of a bitch who ain't even paying him for his time and trouble. Slim was one of the boys who closed in on an old stone cabin up the mountain. Any posse leader with manners would have given old Slim a pat on the back for being so brave. He says Jung cussed him out for taking such a risk and kept riding him, after. Jung is famous for his sarcastic wit. It ain't as amusing to the ones on the receiving end. So old Slim got steamed, told old Whitey to go to hell, and dropped out of the contest. Spud left with him because they're pards, I reckon. I don't know why Whitey Jung talks so mean. Lord knows he's never done anything as all-fired important as he likes to sound off."

Longarm shot the army man a knowing look. "You say you got two hundred dragoons around that mountain, Matt?" he asked.

Kincaid said, "I wish. No company's been up to full strength since the Hayes Administration got so worried about the budget. But my boys aren't allowed to drop out, and I don't think the riders from Grand or Larimer counties will feel as abused as Jung's riders. I only talked to him for a few minutes this afternoon when he came down off the mountain to send some more wires.

26

But Lefty, here, has a point. We used to get second lieutenants like that. I'm sure you've met the type."

Longarm nodded. "I know a short colonel named Walthers who's still a loud-mouthed fool, as a matter of fact. My notes say Deputy Jung is even newer on the job. This would seem to be his first big case. That's likely why he's taking it so serious."

Lefty put down his empty schooner. "He had his chance to call on me for help. I'm heading home afore somebody else can make unkind remarks about me."

As he turned away, Longarm said, "Hold on. I may just be in the market for a decent mount, Lefty."

"That's what we has to offer at the Middle Fork. You want to look the remuda over now?"

"Not in the dark, no offense. One more pair of eyes ain't likely to matter to the north right now and I climb rocks by daylight better after a good night's rest. You say your spread is halfway up to Ward, on this same wagon trace?"

"It is. You can't miss us. We got a sign over our gate. I'll run out some decent stock, knowing we can expect you any time after sunrise. Once we got you mounted decent I'll ride part of the way with you and put you on Skull Trail."

"I thought you said them owlhoots lit out along Dead Cow Creek, Lefty."

"They did. They must not have knowed this country as good as me. Skull Trail is shorter to Long's Peak by half. I'll see you in the morning."

As he clomped out, Kincaid said, "He's right. Skull Trail's the one my dispatch riders are using now. It looks like those strange riders boxed themselves up on Long's Peak through ignorance. What does that do to your ideas about an inside job?"

"Leavenworth wouldn't be so crowded if every crook was smart, or hell, had common sense," Longarm said. "I wouldn't want it to get around, because I like to look good when I run the rascals in, but it's pure statistics that, pound for pound, the criminal population of these United States is stupid as hell. Finish your drink and let's get out of here. I got to find me a safe place to bed down for a few hours."

Kincaid shot a thoughtful glance at the red dress across the room, downed his drink, and said, "You must be tired. Let's go."

Outside, he told Longarm, "There's no hotel or even boarding house in town. My pony is stabled at the smithy. My clerk and I have a tent set up behind the post office. You're welcome to bed down there."

"Won't it be a mite crowded?"

"Not really. We're riding up to Long's Peak as soon as the moon's up enough to matter. I'm planning to use that stone cabin they were talking about as my field headquarters, now that the wires down this way have everyone positioned for me."

Longarm swore. "You might have told me sooner, Matt! I could have rid up with you, and now I've gone and promised to buy a pony off Lefty Page in the morning!"

"That poor brute the remount service stuck you with would never make it up Skull Trail, Longarm," Kincaid said. "You enjoy a good night's rest, get a decent horse, and join us at the stone cabin in the morning. If those outlaws get through me and mine in the moonlight it won't matter, will it?"

Longarm shrugged. "I sort of hope they do. I hate mountain climbing under fire, and if it was up to me we'd just wait the buzzards out."

"With our luck, fall could come late this year. Even if it comes early, we're talking about forty to sixty days, and it's already cold enough on the lower slopes. You know there's no way in hell we can hold such a long line that long."

Longarm sighed and said, "Yeah. That's why I packed my winter underwear. Wouldn't it be funny if, after all this trouble, we find nobody up there?"

Kincaid said he sure had an odd sense of humor. By this time they were back in front of the general store. They unsaddled the poor remount nag and Kincaid said he would tote Longarm's possibles to the tent out back while Longarm got rid of the critter.

Longarm led the weary gelding along the dark and only street to the nearby smithy. It was still early, but the smithy groused about it being the middle of the night when Longarm banged on the wall planks for service. As the smith came out, buttoning up, a pale-faced young woman peeked out at them through the look-see by their side door. She must have thought the glass was even dirtier than it was. She didn't seem to have a stitch on. Longarm said, sincerely, he was sorry about showing up so late with a critter so ugly. The smith said it would cost two bits if Longarm expected the gelding to be oated and watered as well. The price was outrageous, but Longarm paid it. Then he asked if the smith felt up to talking about the shooting out front.

The older man shook his head and said, "I've told the tale to the law, more than once, and there's nothing much to tell. I was hammering out a bent carriage bolt with my back to the street. Lefty Page was lounging in the doorway, pestering me with a story I'd heard afore. I heard Lefty yell and run out, shooting. Time I turned and followed it was all over. Deputy Compten was dying in Lefty's arms whilst the dust was still settling. I never seen the riders passing. Heard 'em, of course. Sounded like half a dozen ponies, steel shod, save for one. A man in my business notices when a pony's running barefoot. Lefty says one was a paint. Likely an Indian pony. Now, if you'll excuse me, I got to tend this horse of your'n so's I can get back to bed, damn it."

Longarm said he could see the smith was anxious to get back under his blankets, and headed back to the scene of the recent crime.

When he worked his way around to the back in the dark he saw that Kincaid and the lance corporal were gathering up their own gear. He said, "You boys better hurry over to the smithy if you don't want some cussing to go with your mounts. It seems our village blacksmith ain't no night owl, despite his strong and sinewy hands."

The lance corporal simpered just like old Henry and said, "Her name is June and they say she's loose. Heard some women gossiping in the store about her this afternoon. They didn't notice me, sitting in the shadows. That old smith figures to wind up dead the day Miss

June's father sobers up enough to notice."

Kincaid said, "That's enough. We're up here to chase bandits, not to gossip about wayward village girls." Then he told Longarm, "I'm leaving our cots and other fold-ups behind. We need our bedding and camping gear. But you'll find some penny candles and a tin of ginger snaps from the store. The water pump's between the tent and Miss Polly's back door."

Longarm asked where that left Miss Polly.

Kincaid laughed. "I might have known you'd ask. She doesn't live there. I don't know where she beds down at night. I don't ask as many nosy questions as you do, pard."

"You don't have to," Longarm said. "You don't pack a badge. I had no idea there was a back door to that post office. I didn't see one inside. Did you?"

Kincaid thought for a moment. "As a matter of fact, no, now that you mention it. There was only one way in or out of the room the robbery took place in. So what's the difference? It's probably how she gets in and out behind her general-store counter. I can't see a lady in long skirts leaping over too often."

Longarm waited until they had left him alone in the back yard. It wasn't fenced in and the aspen rising a few yards farther out grew too raggedly to mark a formal property line. Longarm looked inside the tent, made sure his own gear was where Kincaid had dumped it, and moseyed over to the dark back wall of the one-story frame building to see if there was really a back door.

There was, set near the corner to the east. He tried the knob and wasn't too surprised to find it locked. He

31

got out his pocketknife and opened a blade that could have resulted in arrest had someone less upright been packing such a wicked device. It only took a few moments to unlock the door and open it.

He struck a match. A flight of steps led steeply down into a cellar. The dirt-floored, stone-walled space under the establishment above was filled with stock to be sold upstairs at some future date. He found a ladder going straight up near the front. He climbed it, shoved open the trapdoor at the top, and saw that it led, as Kincaid had guessed, to the space behind the counter. There was nothing suspicious about that, either, so he went back down to see how one could get under that post office safe.

He found one couldn't, from below. He'd thought that safe looked heavy. The cubicle Polly Clark used as the post office in back of her general store was built over solid ground beyond the back wall of her cellar. Only the stairway going down, under the doorway she used above to get into or out of the post office layout, left a bit of the floor above exposed to possible gopher attack. He stood on the steps and tested the flooring above him. It was solid. He shrugged and said, "Hell, everyone *agrees* the rascals come in and left by the front way."

He paused by the yard pump, bent over to water himself a mite as he tried the handle, and went on to the tent. It was earlier than he usually turned in. He feared he might turn in too late if he went back to the only saloon in town to admire Miss Red Robin's awful piano playing and beautiful figure. He lit a penny candle, muttering, "At least they could have left me an army manual. There's nothing like dull reading to put a gent to sleep early."

He lit a cheroot while he was at it. He tossed his hat aside but hadn't even removed his gun rig when he heard someone swishing through the grass outside. He started to snuff the candle, but he didn't, when he heard a familiar female voice call out, "Custis Long, where are you, you brute?"

As she ducked into the tent with him, Longarm said, "Keep it down, Miss Robin. I got my reputation to consider. How come they let you off so early?"

"Nobody lets me do anything. I am a free spirit who does as she likes," she said. Then she dropped to her knees on the grass in front of his cot, her low-cut red velvet gown displaying a great deal in the flickering candlelight, and reached for him as she complained, "I was mad as hell when you and that soldier just turned away and left as if I wasn't there."

He gulped and said, "I figured you'd be on until midnight, as usual, honey. I just come back here to enjoy a smoke and settle my nerves till you got off."

She grinned up at him roguishly. "Goody. But, as you see, I didn't want to wait that long, either. So here I am and—Cuss it, Custis, how come you got on so much underwear?"

"I was planning on clambering over colder parts, not expecting to find you, of all people, halfway up Long's Peak. Let me get my *own* pants off, damn it. Can't you even wait till a man takes off his guns?"

"I wasn't sure you still liked me. If you really do,

33

what say we go to my place? It's been a spell, and I ain't sure that skimpy army cot could handle the two of us."

"You may have a point, if you has more solid walls to offer," he said.

She got to her feet, leaving him unbuttoned, and said, "I got four good walls and a four-poster feath-erbed. Jimtown is about as lonesome a place as I've been since the last time I got out of jail!"

Then she yanked him to his feet as he was reaching to snuff the candle. It was on an inverted tin bucket by the head of the cot and he let it go, knowing it would burn down harmlessly sooner or later. Red Robin led him out by the hand, tugging like a frisky pup on a leash.

"You might have let me put on my fool hat, at least," he said.

"Why put anything on, when you'll only have to take it off so soon? Come on, we can cut through the back yards to my place, and your damned old *hat* isn't what I'm interested in!"

He shot a wistful look back. He could *see* his hat through the wall of the lit-up tent, atop his possibles on the cot. She laughed and said, "It's a good thing you stopped in the nick of time, just now. Anyone stepping out back to take a leak might have got the shock of their life!"

She laughed wickedly. "That's how I knew where you was when you tried to hide, you bashful boy. Oh, hurry, Custis. Ever since I spotted you in the saloon

34

mirror I been thinking back on old times!"

She led him through the back door of a two-story frame house halfway between the post office and the saloon. She got him upstairs, shoved him across a four-poster which took up most of the space in her hired room, and proceeded to peel red velvet.

The pale moon was peeking in through the lace window curtains, painting her voluptuous body with interesting patterns of light as she tossed her gown aside, unpinned her lush hair with her arms up, and asked, "What are you doing with your damned old pants still on, you slowpoke?"

Longarm managed to get rid of his coat, gun rig, and even boots before she was all over him.

He knew, better perhaps than she, why they got along so well together, in bed at least. A warm-natured gal who played piano in saloons got plenty of opportunity for this sort of action. But few riders getting into town, say, once a month could satisfy a woman like Red Robin. But Longarm was a man who tended to rise to a challenge and stay risen.

When they stopped for a breather, she was in a conversational mood. He asked how come he'd found her playing piano in such an out-of-the-way place. "I'd expect to find you in a more interesting town, honey."

She snorted in disgust. "This ain't no town. It ain't even an incorporated village yet. You got here just in time, for tonight would have been my last night even if I hadn't quit early. I was lured up here under false pretenses. I heard rumors of big money in these parts, but so far, the biggest tip I've had dropped in the glass on my piano was two bits."

"I did pass a few small mines or ambitious try-holes, riding up from Lyons today. What sort of color have they been digging hereabouts, Robin?"

She said, "Nothing. The way I hear tell, there's a sometimes vein of gold quartz, mostly quartz, that peters out every time someone gets to digging serious. The mine here in Jimtown opens and closes like a flirty gal's eyelids."

Just then, all hell busted loose outside. Twelve-gauge, from the repeated sound of it.

Red Robin heard the shotgun blasts as well, of course. They were hard to miss. But she told him, "It's nothing. You know how cowhands are when they have nothing better to do."

But he insisted, "Most of the gents in town with guns are supposed to be out on posse right now. Them shots came from close, and I'd best find out how come!"

Longarm didn't bother with his coat, vest, underwear, or socks. He hadn't brought his hat in the first place. He got just decent enough for a quick look-see, strapping on his gun rig as he tore down the stairs.

Out back, folks were running about in the moonlight like headless chickens as Longarm called for some answers. A young kid shouted something about the post office getting robbed again before his mother called him back inside.

Longarm headed for the army tent Red Robin had just dragged him out of. The candle was still burning inside, so he saw the inky outlines of folks standing all about it. As he got closer he saw bright stars of candle-light winking at him where the canvas had been punctured. As he came even nearer, a townie stepped out with Longarm's Stetson in his hand to announce, "Good thing them army men was somewhere else just now. Wonder who this hat belongs to."

Longarm said, "Me," and took his Stetson back before he ducked inside to see what else had been peppered. His saddle and roll had been blown off the cot as well, he saw. A few more modest holes in already well-worn bedding wouldn't hurt enough to matter in high summer. The old McClellan saddle had started out scuffed. The raw spots left by shotgun pellets would hardly show once the rig was saddle-soaped again. But Longarm still felt a certain gratitude to old Red Robin as he considered how much damage the sneaky shooting might have done to his fool hide, had he really been aboard that cot just now.

He put on the Stetson, snuffed the candle, and ducked back outside. "I'd ask which of you might have done the deed if I was dumb enough to think anyone would tell me. I sure hope anyone who saw more than I did just now feels free to talk about it."

There was a lot of confused discussion, but nobody had anything really helpful to offer.

"That's what I figured. Who's the law, here?" he asked.

A man in bib overalls explained, "Whitey Jung's the law, now that old Compten's dead. Jung's up the mountains, looking for the ones as gunned his boss."

Longarm raised an eyebrow and said, "Now that's sort of interesting. Are you saying the town law as got shot by the bandits was the *senior* deputy up here?"

Another townie said, "Sure. Everyone knows that. The sheriff down to Boulder deputized old Compten a couple of years back. Whitey Jung was hired...I dunno, six or eight months ago, I reckon."

There was a murmur of agreement. "Whitey's all right. He just needs time," someone said, and someone else asked, "Don't you mean *brains?* If it had been him and not old Comp they shot, the sons of bitches would be caught by now. Old Comp knew these hills like the palm of his hand."

"That's why I didn't feel like riding with Whitey Jung. That kid don't know his ass from his elbow and it gets *cold* at night up around Long's Peak!" another man put in.

The first townie laughed. "That's what I mean. Who but a fool would think anyone would be fool enough to corner hisself up a peak when he had the whole range to hide in?"

Longarm started to walk away as someone else protested, "Oh, I dunno, boys. The posse did draw fire and they say Slim Tracy did find sign in that old hermit's cabin halfway up."

Longarm felt that anyone who really gave a damn, save for the bastard who'd just tried to gun him, of course, would be with the posse scouting for sign instead of just jawing about it.

He didn't want them pegging shots at Red Robin, either, so he circled some in the dark before he thought it safe to rejoin her. As he dropped his load by the bed in the dark she asked him what it was. He began to unbutton again as he told her, "Saddle, Winchester, possibles. The army is on its own. Now I know why I'm so fond of you, Red Robin. Them shots we just heard were aimed at me, or where I would have been if you hadn't been so smart."

She gasped. "My God! Who was it, Custis?"

He sat down to haul off his boots again. "Well, it wasn't you. After that it gets sort of murky. The easy guess would be one of the bandits who gunned the other lawman, earlier. But if they didn't really ride on and up, like everyone says, I was sent on a fool's errand to begin with, and it would have been sort of foolish to tell me so soon."

As he rolled back into bed with her, she decided, "It was some rascal here in town who was in on the job with them!"

He took her in his arms again. "I already thought about that. If the robbery went like everyone says, it might not have been an inside job. If it was, trying to gun me just now was even dumber. Who'd want to alert me to the dangers of big city life when I figured on leaving in the morning in any case?"

She said, "They may have been more out to kill you than to draw your attention, lover."

"You're smart as well as frisky, honey. Had my fool head been in that hat they spotted through the canvas from outside, it might not have mattered how suspicious someone acted."

"Can we forget about that shotgun, now?" Red Robin

asked. "I want to take up where we left off."

He agreed this was hardly the time for discussing crimes, but he still felt free to keep thinking about his close call, since it had been him they'd been aiming at, neither long ago nor far away. The only thing that seemed obvious was that someone wanted him dead. After that it got harder to figure. He'd been shot at before, usually in an attempt to keep him from finding someone or something out. But unless a lot of others were dead wrong, this case was a simple go-get-'em rather than a job calling for investigative skills. Had it been up to him alone, he'd never have been sent so far to do so little in the first place. For, as all the sign had read, up until that shotgun fusillade just now, a half-dozen simple souls had pulled a simple robbery and lit out with more speed than planning. If they were really boxed in a few miles away, by more riders than it should take to put down a reservation jump, there was nothing *to* the fool case. If the posse had tracked them wrong, they were long gone, and that was that. So why in thunder had someone just tried to kill him?

He rolled Red Robin on her back as he decided aloud, "There's only one answer. There's more to that robbery than meets the eye, and I worried 'em by hanging about the scene of the crime instead of poking about above timberline with everyone else."

Chapter 4

Longarm didn't recall falling asleep in Red Robin's loving arms. But he knew he had when the sound of hoofbeats outside woke him up. He made it over a dozen riders, headed somewhere fast. As he listened he could tell they had ridden in from the east and were now headed west without stopping. Red Robin still lay asleep at his side.

The light through the lace curtains seemed a mite rosy for moonlight. He swung his bare feet silently to the floor and got dressed quietly to avoid waking her up. He knew she would probably be gone by the time he ever passed this way again and her naked curves sure looked tempting by the dawn's early light. But he faced a long ride, so he gathered up his gear and tiptoed out.

The army tent was still there. So were the ginger snaps. He freshened his face with pump water and packed his gear over to the smithy. He felt no guilt about rousting the surly smith out of bed so early.

Longarm banged on the door until the smith opened

up for business and helped him saddle the old army gelding. He asked for directions, just in case, and rode out of Jimtown as the first rooster was crowing. The mountain air was springlike, if one liked cool springs. He followed the wagon trace up some hairpins, with aspen leaves winking green and silver at him to either side, until he spied the lettering burned into a slab of weathered pine and turned in to the Middle Fork spread, on the downhill side of the gravel trace.

Lefty Page was a man of his word who had apparently taken Longarm to be another. Lefty rose from the porch steps where he'd been whittling as Longarm reined in. The ramrod looked the army mount over for a spell before he said, "I give up. What is it?"

Longarm chuckled. "I never said it was a horse." He dismounted and tethered the brute to the porch rail.

Lefty said, "The cook ain't up yet, cuss his hide, but I got coffee on the stove inside, if you're desperate."

"I could use some coffee, but I overslept, too, and I'm in a hurry," Longarm said. "You said you might have something a man could ride here, pard?"

Lefty nodded and led Longarm around to the corral, where four ponies were shivering in the morning cool for his inspection.

Longarm took time to light a smoke as he sized them up. Then he said, "I'll take the strawberry mare."

"You got a good eye for horseflesh. I hope you're brave," Lefty said.

"Oh? She's a bucker?"

"Just a crow-hopper for the first mile or so in the

morning. She means no real harm. We calls her Straw-berry."

"Original name. What are you asking for such a good dancer?"

"With that army mount throwed in?"

"Not hardly. I don't own him. I'll pay you extra if you'll have someone drop him off at South Saint Vrain Remount one of these days."

Lefty pursed his lips. "That's no bother. How do you feel about forty for the mare?"

Longarm scowled at him. "Awful. I might wind up paying out of my own pocket if my office insists the army was good enough to me. Fifteen is about as much as I'm up to risking."

Lefty shook his head. "Can't let you have her for that kind of money. But what if you was to just hire her off us by the day?"

"That sounds less risky than buying a bucker. Two bits a day sound fair, Lefty?"

Lefty shook his head and said, "The Middle Fork's a horse spread, not a livery stable. We generally asks a dollar a day."

"Business must be slow, then. How many greenhorns do you get up here per summer?"

"Fifty cents?" Lefty hazarded.

"Done. I'll get my saddle."

Lefty ran the army mount into the corral and saddled the paint to show Longarm the way to Skull Trail.

Longarm noticed the paint was steel-shod. That didn't mean much, since it had been Lefty who'd told him one of the bandits rode a barefoot Indian. On the other hand, it seemed unlikely a false witness would make up a pony much like the one he seemed to favor for riding himself.

They rode back down the wagon trace to a break in the aspen Longarm had passed getting to the Middle Fork. Lefty reined in and said, "That's her. Stay on the trail and you'll get there sooner or later."

Longarm started to ask why it was called Skull Trail. Then he spotted the first cow skull nailed to a tree. He said, "I heard a mess of other riders, earlier, headed up this way, Lefty. I don't suppose you might have?"

Lefty said, "Nope. If they were riding to join the rest of you up on Long's Peak they'd have turned in here if they knew the way. Otherwise they might have took Dead Cow Creek, even further down."

"You mean I passed that cutoff, too?"

"You must have, since you got this far. You didn't miss much. We calls it Dead Cow Creek because the valley it runs down is sort of soggy, full of ticks and death camus. That's what kills the cows, the death camus. Damn fool cows can't tell death camus from wild onion."

Longarm said he'd heard of greenhorns making the same mistake and they parted friendly. As if she'd waited until Lefty was out of sight, Strawberry tried to take the bit in her teeth and, when that didn't work, she tried to scrape her new rider's kneecap off on a trailside aspen. Longarm cranked her head down, kicked her in the muzzle, and said, not unkindly, "We'd best discuss your manners, Straw-

44

berry. I was told you had a sense of humor. But that wasn't funny. I don't feel like walking ten or more miles any more than you do. So don't make me kill you, and this'll all be over in the sweet by and by."

When he let her head up the mare looked innocent and moved on up the trail more sedately. Skull Trail would have been harder to follow, even with a bleached white cow or horse skull every quarter of a mile or so, had it not been obvious a lot of other riders had been through here recently. Some horse apples were still steaming in the crisp morning air. He wasn't as worried about getting lost as he about getting bushwacked, so he kept an eye peeled despite or maybe because of the short distance one could see. The charred stumps they passed now and again told a tale of a big burn-out in the not-too-distant past. The weedlike aspen, moving in to pioneer new open ground, had sprouted thickly all around. The gray-green aspen trunks and early morning shade made for a sort of zebra-striped wall to either side. It wasn't so clear why the trail wound so much. As a high-plains rider, Longarm was used to riding beeline from here to there unless there was a reason. But wooded trails always seemed to wind, perhaps following the steps of the deer who had first wandered through the woods.

Primed for sight or sound ahead, Longarm was surprised when he heard someone coming up Skull Trail to his rear. It sounded like a rider with business in mind. Longarm reined in, swung Strawberry broadside, and hauled his saddle gun from its boot. He levered a round

45

in the chamber and held the Winchester politely for now.

He was glad he had when a pretty girl on a pretty horse came into view through the second growth. Her mount was a chestnut thoroughbred stud. She was riding him sidesaddle, wearing an Inverness cape over her darker tweed riding habit. A small black derby rode perkily atop her pinned-up chestnut hair. She saw him at the same time and said, "Oh, there you are, I hope. A nice cowboy on a pinto told me the famous lawman, Longarm, just rode up this trail, and I've been trying to catch up with him."

Longarm said, "I don't know how famous I want to act, but you sure caught up with me, Miss . . . ?"

"I'm Wilma Wadsworth of the *Kansas City Star*. They used to call me Weeping Wilma, but I don't write that column any more. I'm out here doing features on the Wild West."

He emptied the chamber of his saddle gun and dropped it back in the boot as he smiled. "I don't know how wild things are up ahead, Miss Wilma, but I'd say you've rid about as far, sidesaddle, as a lady ought to in these parts."

"I'm here intent on covering the big shootout on Long's Peak and you can't fool me. We're nowhere near timberline yet," she said.

He tried not to laugh as he said, "I can see you're an old Rocky Mountain rider, ma'am. I still wish you wouldn't ride much farther. Who told you there was going to be a shootout?"

"That mean Sheriff Love, in Boulder. They just got

word about some outlaws hiding out on Long's Peak and when I asked them to take me along they called me a foolish woman and left without me in the middle of the night. I ask you, was that any way to treat a lady?"

"It might seem more proper than getting her gut-shot," Longarm told her. "Are we talking about a dozen riders or so, ma'am?"

"Yes. I've been following them and following them, all the way up from Boulder. It's a good thing Crusader, here, is a retired racehorse, for I believe those mean things were trying to ditch me. As you might surmise, I'm a determined newspaperwoman once I sense a good story. So their efforts were in vain, unless they took another trail, that is."

Longarm shook his head wearily. "They took this trail, an hour or more ahead of us. I can see you're a determined woman, Miss Wilma, so we'd best make a deal."

She dimpled at him. "Oh, good, what did you have in mind?"

"I'm headed up to join the others surrounding them bandits or nothing much, depending. I can see there's no way of losing you on such a well-marked trail, and the *Kansas City Star* would never forgive me if I lost such a good reporter in this aspen hell to begin with. So you and old Crusader can come along with me and Strawberry as far as the picket line around the mountain. That's providing you savvy that's as far as you want to go. There's a stone cabin there, just as the trail gets seriously steep. Our side will no doubt be using it as a base of operations. You'll find many a lawman there to jaw with. They may know twice as much as I do about the trapped owlhoots by now. I want you to promise me you'll behave yourself and try not to get in the way, once we're close enough to matter. Them gents have enough on their plates right now. I don't ever want it said I brought a pesky female in to add to the confusion."

She said, "I'm not a pesky female. I'm a star reporter for the *Kansas City Star*. Do you want to see my identification?"

"No. A .44-40 would make more sense, where we're headed. I want to get there some time today, so let's get going."

She didn't argue, and he took the lead.

They came to an open glade where a whitewater creek ran through the tall grass like a babbling snake. They reined in to let their mounts sip some snow-melt. They were barely in the woods again before she cleared her throat awkwardly and asked, "Could we stop a moment? I'd like to . . . ah . . . wash my hands."

Longarm reined in, nodded, and suggested, "Don't wash your hands sitting on a fallen log in tick country, ma'am."

If she heard him she didn't answer. She slid gracefully from her sidesaddle and vanished out of sight. Longarm saw that her mount was trained to obey grounded reins. As an experienced traveler, Longarm had learned never to pass up a chance to take a leak. So he dismounted and, not sure Strawberry was trained at all, tethered her to a sapling before he stepped off the trail on the far side.

He was just buttoning up when he heard a distant cry of distress. As he headed her way Wilma Wadsworth was shouting, "Oh, no, *help!*"

When he reached her she was standing, her face red and her dress down, near—what else?—a fallen log.

He tried not to grin as he said, "By the time an aspen grows big enough to fall over like that it's generally rotted and sort of buggy, Miss Wilma."

She wrinkled her nose and replied, "You can say that again. For I fear I'm infested with bedbugs!"

He shook his head. "Wood ticks happen more often than bedbugs up here in the high country, ma'am. I know better than to ask a lady where she's got 'em. But for Pete's sake don't go slapping or picking at 'em. You'll wind up with an infection if you bust off a tick's head under your hide."

She looked sick. "Oh, whatever shall I do?"

He looked away. "There's only two things anyone can do about ticks, ma'am. You can leave 'em be till they fills up with blood and drops off natural, or you can convince 'em to let go some other way."

"You mean you have some bug powder I could sort of use in private?"

"No, ma'am. I ain't even packing larkspur lotion in my possibles. But I do have plenty of smokes. If you hold a lit cheroot end about where a tick's shoulders would be, if a tick had any shoulders, they let go and back out to get away. That's when you stomp 'em, of course."

She regarded him warily. "I don't smoke."

He fished out a cheroot, lit it, got it going good with

49

a few strong puffs, and held it out to her, saying "Here you go. I'd best go back to the horses whilst you do what must be done."

She took the cheroot, holding it by the end as if she feared it might explode. "What if I burn myself?" she asked.

He shrugged. "Little old burn won't damage you as much in the end as an infected tick head. You want me to do it for you?"

"Good heavens, no! What sort of a girl do you take me for?"

"A greenhorn gal who's likely to wind up with ferocious festers in the near future if she don't wise up, sudden."

It hardly seemed possible her face could get any redder, but it did as she said, "Oh, Lord, they told me it was wild out here. But this is just awful. Can I trust you to act like a gentleman in every other way?"

He said, "It might help if you was to think of me as a sort of doctor. You'd be surprised at some of the doctoring I've had to do in my time."

"No, I wouldn't," she said, but she handed him the smoke and turned around to hoist her skirt and bend over. "Try not to look at anything but those creatures, please."

He tried, but it would have been easier had she been wearing underdrawers. Like lots of women forced to dress stuffy in high summer, Wilma had no doubt assumed an ankle-length skirt would get her by in mixed company and, until about now, it likely had. Longarm dropped to one knee behind her and proceeded to back

50

about half a dozen ticks out of her soft, creamy skin. She flinched and told him he was burning her.

"No, I ain't. I'm burning bugs. Got to almost brand you whilst I'm at it. But I won't, if you'll just hold *still*."

She couldn't, but he only blistered her once in the end as the last tick came out to die between his horny fingers. His fingers weren't the only horny parts of him as he said, "That's the last one. You can drop your skirt now, ma'am."

She did, still facing away from him as he wiped his fingers with an aspen leaf. "Oh, how can I ever face you now?" she said.

He said, "Turning around would be a start. I'm going back to the trail, now. Why don't you compose yourself and follow in your own good time, ma'am? I can wait . . . a reasonable time, that is."

He began to wonder how long that might be as he smoked what was left of his cheroot aboard Strawberry. He was beginning to wonder if she'd gotten lost in the woods when she finally came out of them, still red-faced, but laughing.

"Well, nobody can ever say I didn't see the Wild West, and vice versa. I fear you must think I'm awfully silly," she told him.

As she mounted up, Longarm shook his head. "You ain't silly, ma'am. You're just green. A greenhorn as can't admit to being green can get silly—or dead—out here. But I never laugh at folks' mistakes unless they go on making the same ones."

As they rode on she said, "You're a very understand-

51

ing person, Deputy Long. Somehow I don't feel as ridiculous, now, as I know I really *should* be feeling."

He shrugged. "I felt ridiculous the first time I tried to rope a calf when I come West after the War. After a spell I got the hang of it. But I never forgot the feeling. So I try not to laugh at ladies and gents whose only mistake is being younger than me. None of us are born knowing everything."

She sighed. "I guess I still have a lot to learn. You say you were in the War, sir? My father was in the War, fighting for the Stars and Bars."

He grimaced and said, "I disremember which side I was riding for when your dad and me was younger and no doubt more foolish."

"Oh, I'm sure he was a little older than you. You must have been just a boy at the time."

"All of us started out boys, ma'am. Those of us who came back alive felt somewhat older by the time it was over. Could you call me Custis and change the subject, Miss Wilma? Like I said, we all feel smarter as we ripen some, and I don't like to dwell on my misspent youth."

She fell silent. He didn't know whether she was being polite or feeling hurt. He feared he might have been too short with her. He knew why, if he had. For it had been in woods much like these, green and pretty, he'd had to kill another young and foolish boy. The first man he'd ever killed, if one could count such a baby-faced kid a man. Longarm seldom felt bad about gunning an outlaw, but he'd often wondered, over the years, what that other boy at Shiloh would have grown up to be if he'd fired first. That beardless face had stared back at him so innocent and surprised as he'd come unstuck and fired first after that long horrible eternity of mutual buck-fever. And then it had been time to move on through the smoke-filled woods and then he was meeting others, and not hesitating, and by sundown a grown man called Private Long had come out the other side, even if he wouldn't be shaving regular for a while.

He figured the girl riding behind him now would have been eight or ten the bloody day he became a man all at once. That was likely why she still thought of her daddy's Stars and Bars as a gallant banner instead of a grim miscalculation. He knew some females were bothered by the way he sometimes fell silent for a spell. So he called back cheerfully, "I see more daylight up ahead."

"Are we getting up to the timberline, then?" she called back, too brightly.

"Not yet. These aspen have to give way to fir trees first. Looks like a mountain meadow, though."

It was. As they came out of the trees she gasped, "Oh, how lovely!" and he had to admit the scene looked fair enough, in summer, at least. For forty acres or so of stirrup-high flowers spread all around a placid blue pond in the middle, with an old log cabin, overgrown with red roses, on the far side.

She asked if he thought anyone lived there. He shook his head and said, "Not now. They'd have trimmed that rambling rose more often if they'd stayed long after planting it. Look what it's doing to the roof shakes. I'd say someone settled here just long enough to see there wasn't enough color in the rocks all about to matter. Wasn't a stock spread. Not enough grazing for that. These mountains are full of old deserted dwellings. Folk out here are restless. Let's ride on."

She asked, "Can't we look inside? I feel sure this old cabin has many a story to tell, if only it could speak."

"It can't," he said, but reined in to indulge her. She dismounted and ran in like a little kid. He was curious enough to follow her. But there was little to see inside. The one-room cabin had been stripped. Anything on the dirt floor anyone might have missed had long since been taken by the pack rats. Or at least the pack rats *should* have. He bent to pick up a pistol round. He mused, "Unfired. .36 Colt, made for a converted Navy Colt. It's brand new. The bullet, not the gun it was purchased for. Pack rats should have admired it by now if it lay there more than a night or so."

"Do you think one of those bandits we're after could have dropped it?" she asked.

"Somebody did, reloading in the dark, most likely. But them owlhoots are said to have taken the other, rougher trail. *We* ain't after them, by the way. I told you you get to ride as far as the posse line and no farther." He put the evidence in his coat pocket and added, "Let's go. There's nothing else here worth looking at."

"It looks so sad. I'm sure some woman who loved roses must have planted that one out front. Whatever must have happened to her, Custis?" she asked.

He shrugged. "Can't rightly say. They wasn't hit by Indians. They had time to pack. Don't waste no tears on a gal who could be living high on the hog in a bigger

54

house today, for all we know."

They went outside and remounted. As they rode away Wilma looked back wistfully and said, "I hope they found whatever they were looking for, in time. It must have hurt to leave such a dear little place."

He didn't think she wanted to hear what the winters could be like up here in a one-room shack. They rode on through more aspen and then the timber got more spaced out as they climbed higher into spruce and fir. They rode downhill a spell. Mountain trails were like that. As they started climbing again, Longarm glanced up at a suddenly darker sky and said, "We'd best break out our slickers, ma'am. Looks like thunder on the mountain coming, pronto."

He turned in his saddle to do so. She looked stricken. "Oh, I didn't pack a raincoat. Should I have?" she asked.

He nodded. "Nobody goes up in the Front Range, come summer, without a slicker. Present company aside, I mean."

Then a big fat frog hopped off his hatbrim with a happy splash and he added, "Here, you'd best put my slicker on. I'll wrap up in my bedroll tarp."

She drew up alongside him, protesting it hardly seemed fair to him. Just then a lightning bolt split a nearby tree to the roots and Strawberry decided it was time to test her wings. She might have bucked higher had not Wilma been aboard as well. For her own way of spooking at lightning had been to wrap both arms around Longarm and hang on tight.

He'd as quickly grabbed her around the waist to keep

her from falling between their rapidly separating mounts. He had no choice but to hang on to a screaming human female with one arm while he hung on to Strawberry with the other for the duration of her rain dance.

It was raining fire and salt and all of them were soaking wet by the time Longarm had things more under control. They were off the trail, backed into a clump of blue spruce, as he was able to lower the gal to the ground and twist his bucker's head in a way even Strawberry could savvy as a rider who'd had just about enough. Lightning bolts were coming down almost as fast as the rain now. Longarm rolled out of the saddle to grab Strawberry's muzzle and steady her while the terrified girl tried to climb him like a tree, sobbing, "I can't stand it! Make it stop!"

He put a comforting free arm around her. "I would if I could, ma'am. This does feel something like an artillery barrage, but it'll soon be over. The old thunderbird don't hang about long up here. He just *sounds* like he never means to leave till he gets you."

A nearby tree was blown to slivers and she buried her wet face in his wet chest to scream down his vest pocket. He hugged her closer. "We're in a saddle between two rises. We ought to make it," he said.

"What about that tree?" she gasped.

"It's what you get for growing so tall," he said. "I'm taller than you and you don't hear me bawling, do you?"

A million wet years later the rain slacked off. The thunderbird lashed a few more high spots for luck and then flew on to scare the hell out of others. He said,

"See? What did I tell you? It's over and we're still alive, even if we do figure to die of pneumonia if we don't get dried out soon. Come on, let's go see how Crusader made out."

The thoroughbred hadn't made out well at all. Longarm was in front, leading Strawberry on foot as the shivering girl got to ride back up the trail on his saddle. When Longarm saw what had happened he handed the reins to Wilma. "Stay here. It ain't pretty," he told her.

Then he drew his pistol and moved on up to see if the burned horse needed to be put out of his misery.

Crusader was stone-cold dead. The lightning had split him from hindquarter to one front hoof. Longarm grimaced, got the big dead horse free of saddle and bridle, and carried them back to where Wilma had reined in, too close. Her face was ashen but she was trying to be brave, now, as she asked, "Is he?"

Longarm said, "Yep. Hang on to your gear, will you? I'll have to lead you the hard way from here on. It can't be too far, now. Lightning don't get that serious till you're approaching timberline."

Chapter 5

He was right, in the end, but it felt like he'd walked forever with wet socks by the time they were crossing a sunny slope dotted here and there with little junipers and covered everywhere with what looked like railroad ballast. Tufts of grass and alpine saxifrage sprouted here and there where the frost-shattered granite gave anything else room to spread out. Wilma gazed all about in wonder and asked, "Where's Long's Peak? I don't see any mountain up here taller than the others all around."

"That's because we're *on* Long's Peak, not looking at it from a distance," he said. "The real crest is hidden by all the hogbacks ahead. Think of us as ants in a rock garden and you'll have a better picture. It's the pebbles us ants are closest to that take up our eyesight. But don't worry. We're about three-quarters of the way up the mountain, I hope. Sure is a big old bump, ain't it?"

"Where are the other men up here, surrounding those bandits on the summit?" she asked. "Higher, of course," he said. "It would take the whole U.S. Army to form a circle this far down the old peak's skirts. They say there's a cabin where the climb commences to get serious. You'll be able to dry out there, if they have a fire going. I for one will be mad as hell if they don't."

She said, "I'm goosebumps all over. Couldn't we stop and build a fire here? It can't be that late, and I don't see how I could ever take these wet clothes off in front of so many strange men!"

He started to say something really stupid. Then he led Strawberry off the trail toward a big clump of rounded boulders as he told her, "Ought to be warmer, yonder, with the sun from the southwest."

He led her into a sort of hollow nest where wood ash told a tale of others using such a handy rock shelter in the past. He helped her down and suggested, "Spread your wet duds flat on the granite to dry while I see if I can scout up some kindling."

She gulped and said, "Custis, I'm wearing nothing under this riding habit, as well you know."

He nodded. "This was your notion, and it ain't like you got all that many secrets to hide from an old tick-picking pal."

She laughed. "Well, as long as you promise to be good."

He didn't answer. He'd about recovered from Red Robin. But on the other hand he wanted to get up to that posse line sometime before it fell apart. So he moved out on the open slope to see if they'd left him any firewood.

He found a dead juniper branch here and an old root there until he had good armful. Looking down, he didn't see the two riders coming up the mountain until they were almost within pistol range. That was something to consider. So he dropped his load and drew his pistol as he studied their approach.

They reined in at loud conversing distance and one called, "Hold your fire, cowboy. We're law. U.S. Postal Inspectors. You with the posse?"

Longarm called back, "Not yet. I'm law, too. Justice Department. I reckon we're after the same post office robbers."

The older and meaner-looking post office man scowled and yelled back, "The hell you say! *We* have jurisdiction on such cases, Justice. Who in thunder told you this was any business of your department?"

"My department," Longarm said. "Do I look dumb enough to volunteer? I was sent from Denver yesterday by Marshal Billy Vail. You may have noticed how long it takes to get up this fool hill. How long have you boys been at it?"

"Not that long. We just heard about the robbery last night. What's this about Denver hearing earlier? We ride out of the *Boulder* post office!"

Longarm shrugged. "Don't look at me. I just work here."

The mean-faced one said, "No, you don't. It's our case, not yours. They had no right to send you. So you'd best just turn around and head back for Denver. I mean it."

Longarm was still holding his gun polite. His tone was less courteous as he replied, "I don't take my orders from a Postal Inspector. I work for U.S. Marshal Billy Vail, and he told me to come up here. So that's where I am. Your move."

The more civilized-looking inspector nudged the ornery one. "Come on, Hamp. There's no bandits *here,*" he said.

Hamp stared thoughtfully at Longarm as he replied, "Maybe not. But this mule-head from Justice seems to be *calling* me, Gus."

"Oh, for God's sake, Hamp. They sent us to hunt them robbers, not to pick a fight with other fools," Gus said.

Hamp stared hard at Longarm. "How about that, fool? Do you feel I'm trying to pick a fight with you?"

Longarm said, "I can't say, yet. Picking is one thing. Fighting can be another thing entire. It's still your move, pard."

Hamp left his .45 right where it was, but growled, "Well, as long as you don't ride no closer, then. Speaking of riding, I don't see your mount. How come?"

Longarm said, "She's drying out, not far from here. We got wet in the thunderstorm, coming up. You boys must have been quicker with your slickers. So, if it's all the same to you, I mean to build a dry-out and I'll join you all later, up yonder."

"Not if you know what's good for you," snapped Hamp. Then his sidekick said something softer and they rode on, the louder one still cursing.

Longarm regathered his kindling and strode across the slope to rejoin Wilma and Strawberry among the rocks. He almost dropped his kindling when he saw how much the gal had been hiding under her riding habit. She was covering her breasts coyly with her crossed arms, but there was plenty of soft nude flesh left over.

"I feel better already. The thin air up here is so dry and the sun is surprisingly warm among these rocks, out of the wind," she said.

"That's why I brought you here." He knelt beside her and proceeded to build a fresh fire on the ashes of the old one. As soon as he got it going he told her, "Keep this going while I unsaddle Strawberry and rub her down."

As he turned his back to her she asked, "What about you? You look chilled to the bone. Aren't you uncomfortable?"

"Yep. So's this mare, and she can't do nothing about it. That's why horses have to come first. You'd know that if it had been you instead of your daddy, riding for *any* flag."

He tossed the saddles over a boulder to dry, rubbed Strawberry as dry as he could with a damp saddle blanket, and left her to nibble rock garden blooms before he spread a dry blanket from his bedroll on the ground near the naked lady and shucked most of his wet duds. As he spread them out on a warm rock next to hers Wilma said, "That's not fair. You *were* wearing underdrawers and now I really feel naked."

He reclined at her side with his gun handy and a fresh smoke gripped in his grin as he told her, "Women have less to hide, and you asked me to be good, remember?"

She dimpled. "Oh? And don't you think you *could* be good if you took those damp drawers off, Custis?"

"Nope. I'm only human, and you're pretty as hell, even with your ankles covered."

She lay back to luxuriate in the sun, fully exposing her naked charms as she closed her eyes and murmured, "You can take your drawers off, now. I won't peek."

He muttered, "Enough is enough, Lord. Nobody can ever say I never tried," as he peeled himself down.

A moment later Wilma's eyes were open indeed as she stared up at him and gasped, "Custis! What on earth do you think you're doing?"

He kissed her and wedged her cool thighs farther apart as he asked mildly, "You mean you can't *tell?*"

She giggled despite herself. "You promised to be good." Then she gasped and groaned, "Oh, Lord, you *are* good, and that feels so *good!*"

He kissed her and said, "I was just now told to go no farther."

She blinked in surprise. "What are you talking about? You must have guessed I've been wanting you to go this far since we first met, you gorgeous cowboy of my dreams!"

"You're pretty, too. I ain't no cowboy any more. I'm the law. Two other lawmen just told me they don't want me on the case. I have to study on just whose case it might be. But we may as well let 'em settle in and simmer down, some, before we catch up with 'em. Hamp may feel safer if there's soldiers and other lawmen about when next we meet. He sure was a proddy cuss."

"Do we have to talk about anything right now, dear?"

They didn't. But an hour later their duds were reasonably dry and he was feeling guilty about the owlhoots up the mountain. So they got up and dressed.

She agreed her hired sidesaddle would be safe enough there for now. So he got to ride the rest of the way up with Wilma riding pillion behind him, clinging tighter than she really had to to keep from falling off.

As was only to be expected on a complicated mountain, they rode over a rise before they spotted the stone cabin nestled in a one-sided hollow below. A steep slope rose above the low-pitched roof and smoking chimney to one side. The other side faced an alarming slope to nowhere. Longarm said, "I can see why it's deserted, now. One morning someone stepped out to take a leak and fell into a cloud."

As they rode down the incline toward the other horses all about the cabin, Captain Matt Kincaid came out to hail them. Once Longarm reined in and helped Wilma down Kincaid said, "We've been expecting you. What took you so long? A couple of Post Office men said they passed you on the trail over an hour ago."

Longarm introduced Wilma Wadsworth to the officer, then asked, "Where would old Hamp be about now, Matt? You may have to sort of referee a jurisdictional dispute."

Kincaid nodded. "They told me. They've moved on up the mountain after leaving word I was supposed to keep you here, or some such nonsense."

Then he paused as a blue-clad dragoon packing red and white signal flags slid down the slope behind the cabin to join them, saying "Message from Post Three, sir. Sergeant Flannery wants to know what to do about conflicting civilian orders."

Kincaid frowned. "Nobody gives us orders. What's Flannery so mistaken about?"

The signalman said, "You know them two sets of sheriff's deputies over that way, sir? Well, one bunch wants Flannery to arrest the other bunch for him, and the sarge thought you'd want to know."

Kincaid rolled his eyes heavenward. "Go back up and signal our men to pay no attention to dumb civilians and await further instructions from me. Sooner or later I may be able to figure some out."

The young soldier turned and ran to scramble back up to his post. Longarm asked what in thunder was going on.

Kincaid said, "I wish I knew. We were requested by a Deputy Eric Jung, right?"

"Close enough. They call him Whitey. So what, Matt?"

"A few hours ago another mess of lawmen rode up here under an Under-Sheriff Love. He seems to be crazy, too."

"Oh, I know Sheriff Love," Wilma said. "He ditched me in Boulder. He's in charge of things up here, he says."

Kincaid looked pained and said, "So he just told us. Deputy Jung doesn't seem to agree at all. They're both a mile or so around the mountain, I hope, arguing about who gets to arrest any bandits who may or may not be up here with us."

Longarm frowned. "I can see how you and me got dragged in, Matt. I got to read the wire early yesterday. I wonder how come an under-sheriff in Boulder got the news a good twelve hours or more later. Boulder ain't half as far from here as Denver."

"Love's not only wondering, he's mad as a wet hen about it," Kincaid said. "He seems to feel a junior deputy is trying to steal his case from him. He says this is Boulder County and that Jung had no call to yell for us without at least dropping a line to the county seat about that robbery in Jamestown."

Longarm sighed. "I've worked with eager pups in my day. That explains why the Post Office is so broody, too. Old Whitey didn't go through channels. He ain't been a deputy long enough to know that's impolite. He wants all the glory to himself. New deputies can sure act ambitious if you don't sit on 'em."

Wilma said, "Wait, I have to get my notepad out so I can get some of this down on paper." As she reached in her bag tied to Longarm's saddle she continued, "Let's see if I have this right. Are you gentlemen saying there's a serious jurisdictional dispute here?"

Longarm told her, "I wouldn't call it serious. Me and old Matt, here, are grown men. The War Department sent him and his men. The Justice Department sent me. Neither one of us will cry if someone else catches the cussed owlhoots. But the Post Office and County Sheriff's Department seem to feel left out. Meanwhile it ain't getting any earlier, and nobody with a lick of sense will climb much higher if someone don't get cracking soon."

67

Kincaid suggested they all go inside and coffee up. The interior of the spacious stone-walled cabin looked as if it had been bare before the army moved in. The same owl-eyed clerk was jawing around the fireplace with a couple of army dispatch runners until they all popped to attention. Kincaid put them at ease with a weary smile and led Longarm and the girl to a trestle table. One of the soldiers came right over with tin cups and a pot of coffee. That was the way a good officer ran an outfit. As they settled down Kincaid told Longarm, "There's more than one way to look at this dumb situation, Custis. If what Love says is true, that junior deputy wasn't authorized to call on your department or mine for help, right?"

Longarm inhaled some coffee, aware his words were being taken down in shorthand by the now prim and proper woman reporter. He said, "I don't take my orders from Boulder County. Whether my own boss knew what he was doing or not, he ordered me to come up here and give Jung's posse a hand."

Kincaid nodded and said, "That's how me and mine wound up here, too. But if Jung's not really in charge—"

"Them bandits is still running loose," Longarm cut in. "Old common law is clear on that point. It's the common duty of all law-abiding citizens to try and stop a crime in progress and until them rascals is caught, they're in progress. I've never understood all this talk about jurisdiction. Maybe that why I've wound up in Mexico or Canada a few times and to hell with jurisdiction. A lawman's job is to catch lawbreakers. That's what I come up here to do, and we can argue about the fine points later."

As it turned out, it was later than Longarm thought. Just then the door burst open and the two Postal Inspectors came in. The milder-mannered one said, "We came under fire just a little way up the trail. So they're there."

The one called Hamp spotted Longarm. "I thought I told you to butt out of our case, Justice."

"We was just talking about jurisdiction, gents," Longarm said. "Won't you join us?"

Hamp said, "Go ahead and finish your coffee. For then you'll be leaving if you know what's good for you!"

Longarm rose slowly from the table to mildly ask, "What do think is good for me, you loud-mouthed stamp-licking bag of brag?"

Kincaid snapped, "That's enough! Both of you! I'll not have a shootout in my infernal orderly room, damn it!"

Longarm asked wistfully, "Can't I just stomp him, then?"

"No. I mean it, Longarm!" Kincaid said.

Hamp's eyes widened as he took a step backward. "Christ! Is this gent the one they call *Longarm?*"

Longarm shook his head at Kincaid and muttered, "Spoilsport."

Kincaid nodded up at Hamp. "It is, and now you have something to tell our grandchildren about, don't you?"

Across the table from him, Wilma asked, "Custis, why do they call you that?"

In the bluff way bullies usually tried to repair such damage Hamp told her, "He's considered the long arm of the law, ma'am." Then he held out his hand. "Put her there, pard. You should have told us Justice was taking this case so seriously."

Longarm didn't shake. "Let's talk about who run you boys back down the mountain," he said.

Gus Polk said, "We moved up the trail afoot. You can't ride much farther before it gets too spooky. It was steep enough where they stopped us. Put a rifle ball between us with a sheer drop to our east and no cover but sheer rock to our left. We slid back around the hairpin sudden to ponder our next move. There may be another way up. They got that one nailed shut."

Hamp said, "It'll be too dark in a little while, anyway."

Kincaid glanced at the glassless window across from him. "I dunno. I'd say there's a good four hours of light left to work with."

Hamp shook his head. "A body might be able to make the top in that time with nobody pegging shots at him. But he'd still have to get back down, in the dark, and we're talking *steep* once you work around the first few bends above here."

Kincaid grimaced. "I was sure looking forward to yet another night up here, even if it is August. But if we can't get up, we'll just have to wait for the rascals to come down."

Longarm lit a smoke, wishing Wilma would stop writing everything down. "Well, I have my sheepskin coat. But I dunno. Seems to me a man could creep about over even steep rock better in the bullet-proofing of night. We're talking a lot of slope to cover, and there has to be more than one way up or down, Matt."

"They took the only way my map says a horse can negotiate, and then not all the way to the top," Kincaid told him.

Wilma asked, "How do you know they still have their horses with them?" Then she blushed, as even she could see the answer.

The blustering Hamp must have wanted to make up some more. He said, "I can answer that, little lady. We know they didn't leave their ponies behind because nobody found no ponies up here. The trail Gus and me followed was wide enough to hold a horse. A skinny one, at least. We figure they have their mounts penned up in some scoop-out, farther up the trail. Long's Peak is busted up ferocious. They say there's flat parts even up near the crest. One side's steep as anything. The other slope's more gentle."

"They didn't ride up the gentle side," Kincaid said. "Not if they just fired on you from the cliff side. But you're right about the ponies. They couldn't be far up that trail." He called his company clerk over. "Corporal, I want a five-man diamond posted a couple of bends up the trail I hope you just heard us talking about. Tell them to dig in and brace for an after-dark mounted bust-out. Any questions?"

"Yes, sir. We don't have five men here, sir."

"You just noticed? Go tell Thompson to wave them

in from Flannery. Signal Flannery to spread what's left of his platoon to cover the gaps. What are you waiting for, a kiss goodbye?"

The corporal dashed out as if the cabin was on fire. Longarm chuckled. Old Matt had been like that when the Cheyenne were acting up, too.

Longarm said, "Well, we got our blankets and plenty of grub, which I hope is more than them owlhoots up the mountain can say."

He didn't see why that should make old Wilma blush like that, but women were always hard to figure.

Kincaid said something about supper. Then the door burst open again and a tall jasper with short-cropped hair so blond it could be mistaken for white came in to complain, "I've had enough! Nobody talks to *me* like that!"

Kincaid said, "Longarm, this is Deputy Whitey Jung. I don't know what he's sore about, either."

Jung said, "Well, I surely do. That infernal Under-Sheriff Love just yanked my badge, and so me and mine are heading home!"

Kincaid gasped. "You can't take your *riders* with you! We don't have enough men up here to keep those outlaws bottled as it is!"

"The hell you say! Sorry, ma'am," Jung snarled. "The boys with me was deputized by me and, if I go, they go. And, as of this cotton-picking minute, I'm *gone!*"

Chapter 6

By suppertime the old stone cabin seemed mighty crowded, when one considered how many men had left the mountain.

Under-Sheriff Love from Boulder took up more than his share of room and army grub while he made enough noise for at least two army mule skinners. He was a big bluff man with a big .44 and a wide sombrero. Some might have found his hat more amusing if Love hadn't looked so tough. Longarm began to suspect he was dumb as well, as the cuss went on and on about having Deputy Jung's badge.

Longarm and Wilma Wadsworth were sitting on his rolled up bedding in as far a corner as they'd been able to find, eating army coffee and drinking army beans. As the loudmouth carried on, Longarm observed more quietly, "He's likely to have a time making that charge stick, since old Whitey never pulled out before Love told him he was fired. Whether an under-sheriff has the power to do that or not is up for grabs. But if I wanted to hold a posse together I suspect I'd start by talking nice to it."

"He brags too much for a man who knows his job," she said. "I just got out here and I can see Deputy Jung and his own riders had to be sort of close and clannish, growing up together in the same community and all."

He started to tell her she was wrong, but he decided, "Close enough, I reckon. Not too many white kids have been born in these parts, yet, to have grown up together. Less than twenty years ago this was still pure Indian country, red rambler roses and all. But folks make friends out here sudden, if they mean to stay out here long, alive. Whitey would have recruited riders more used to him and Jimtown. Mostly cowhands off surrounding spreads. Boys working for the same outfit any length of time at all do get tight. You have to trust another man when you're working the same rugged range and burning ticks off one another from time to time."

She giggled. "That is a good way to break the ice, isn't it? But I'd better take some notes for my story about less scandalous Wild West customs. Are you serious about the short time you seem to think this country has been settled?"

"I don't think. I know," he said. "Twenty years ago Denver was a gold camp along Cherry Creek. By the time I got out here after the War the wild cherries had all been cut for firewood and they had the main streets paved. Folks learn to work hard and move fast out this way if they expect to get along."

She frowned thoughtfully. "I'll take your word on

Denver. But back in Jamestown everything looked so old and rundown one could swear it had been there forever."

He nodded. "Cheap lumber, not enough nails, and jerry-built to begin with. Unpainted wood weathers fast. That's why folk paint barns and whitewash fences when they have the time and money. The mining around Jimtown is sort of casual. Raising stock up here in the mountains ain't as profitable as it is on the old buffalo grounds to the east, neither. So such population as Jimtown might have depends on petty cash from small mines that only stay open long enough for the new owners to figure they was salt-sold. Or maybe hiring on extra during roundup time. The small mountain spreads are mostly run family, with no more than half a dozen on the regular payroll. Nobody with a lick of sense tries to hold a really big herd together on such busted-up range."

She wrinkled her pert nose. "Poor things. I did get that impression things were sort of bleak up here. I wasn't sure till just now whether all the faded jeans and battered hats were meant as poverty or local color."

He said, "Both. Duds weather fast in thin air, cruel sunlight, and ferocious climate. Some, at least, have been making enough to leave cash in a post office safe until someone's dumb enough to build a bank in an unincorporated hamlet."

She sighed. "I imagine those robbers got just about all they had to show for a lot of hard work, then."

He nodded grimly. "That's what we're all doing up

on this otherwise uninteresting mountain, honey. Robbing a train or a bank is bad enough. The gang we're after acted just plain *mean.*"

He paused to light an after-supper smoke as she wrote that down. Then she said, "I'd better get something about the Indians as well."

"There ain't none," he said. "I told you that rose-covered cottage we passed hadn't been burnt out by Indians, remember?"

"I still can't believe that ruin could be younger than me, or even you," she said. "I remember you just said this used to be Indian country, Custis."

He nodded. "Used to be ain't this evening. The natives who called these hills the Shining Mountains didn't suffer too much from the early mountain men. They just got their complexions lightened some, swapping squaws and beaver pelts for gunpowder, salt, and firewater. But when our kind struck Colorado *gold* back in the sixties, whites from all over creation tore through these mountains like there had to be color under every rock. When you consider how out-of-the-way a lot of mountain mining towns wound up, it seems safe to assume the gold rushers looked everywhere. You must know how hard it is to keep uneducated, hard-drinking whites from fighting amongst themselves. Add illiterate Indians full of firewater to the lethal brew and the results are predictable as tossing a lit match in a powder keg."

She said, "Oh dear, how come we never heard of that Indian war back East?"

"There wasn't what a fair-minded fighting man

would call a war. To have a war you have to have sort of even numbers," he told her. "Don't tell old Matt Kincaid—he's bucking for major before he retires—but us whites have the edge on Indians when it comes to slaughter. Poor old Red Cloud had us outnumbered better than ten to one and he still lost in the end. Last I heard of Quanna Parker he was living white down Texas way, and he once led a hell of a mess of Comanche. The Utes, Arapaho, and such of Colorado was brave, but they never had the *numbers* to stand up to all the whites crowding in on 'em at once. They tried. Official history books now give the dates on so-called battles and massacres, but they were mostly short-lived squabbles, like the Apache to the south go in for. When a couple of Indians got killed it went down as a battle. When a handful of Utes jumped a smaller party of whites it was a massacre, of course. Most Utes are pent-up miles from here now. The Arapaho got to share their reserve with South Cheyenne, farther east."

"Which were around here, then, Arapaho or Ute?" she asked.

He blew a thoughtful smoke ring. "I ain't sure. Locals speak of a sort of mysterious band they call Kimoho. Some say that means something like 'Friendly Utes'. You can't prove it by me. They'd been driven out, friendly or not, by the time I got out west, years ago. Last time I was up this way an older white lady showed me some baskets she said Kimoho women had given her for being nice to them. She said she and her man had never had trouble with the Kimoho and that she thought they'd got a raw deal. The basketwork looked Ho, as Utes call themselves. I've always found Ho in general easy to get along with. Come to think of it, a lot of trouble might have been avoided if they'd sent me instead of Terry to powwow with the Lakota Confederacy."

She stared at him in wonder. "Good heavens, were you involved in Custer's Last Stand, too?"

He smiled thinly. "Not hardly. I still got all my hair. But me and Matt Kincaid, over there by the fire, got to sort of clean up after Terry, Crazy Horse, and other hasty gents. The army borrowed me off Justice as a scout. Old Matt and his dragoons listened to advice better than old Terry. So, like I said, it was sort of one-sided. Less'n two years after Terry got Custer's command butchered, we had the whole confederacy reserved."

She was scribbling furiously. "Oh, I've always wanted to do a piece on Custer! You must tell me all about that terrible mistake he made at Little Bighorn!"

Longarm looked disgusted. "It wasn't *his* mistake, it was General Terry's. Custer, Reno, and Benteen were out on point, following Terry's orders, no matter what they thought of 'em."

"Then it was Terry who was the greenhorn?"

"Yes and no. To be fair, everyone on our side, including Crow scouts who knew the country, figured they was only after Red Cloud and his modest band. Nobody knew Red Cloud's sort of Indian Pope, Sitting Bull, had called a council of all the Lakota allies and some as didn't even like 'em. So while Terry's screening force had more than enough riders to deal with what they *thought* they'd been ordered to round up, when they met the enemy the odds were more like ten to one."

He took another drag. "Custer didn't do anything Reno and Benteen didn't. Everyone followed standard military tactics that day. Reno and Benteen made a stand and held their ground for forty-eight fighting hours. Custer and his men got hit the hardest and couldn't. That's why Reno and Benteen ain't as famous today. They was in the same battle, but they kept their hair. Can we change the subject, now? I never come all the way up this mountain to tell war stories. It's starting to get fair dark out, now. As soon as you get sleepy you can use this roll we're sitting on."

She batted her lashes at him in the soft firelight and asked, "In *here,* dear? It surely won't get *that* private in here even if they let the fire go out."

He nodded. "They won't. I want you bedded down here because there's safety in numbers and it might rain again this side of sunrise. Sky outside is clear, but the air feels sort of wet for this high and time of the year."

She insisted, "Never mind about the *weather,* darn it! How are we to . . . you know, with all these others crowded in with us?"

He smiled at her fondly. "We can't. Couldn't if we wanted to. I don't mind confessing I feel mighty wistful about that. I won't be here. I got me a mountain to climb."

She gasped. "You can't be serious! Those other lawmen only got a few yards up the trail before someone shot at them!"

He nodded and said, "I've been considering some

time. I may be loco, but it seems to me I'd rather have someone shooting at me in the *dark* than the *other* way. We got to settle this matter before them owlhoots find out we don't have enough guns up here to hold 'em if they try a go-for-broke bust-out."

She clutched at him and protested, "I won't let you take such a risk, you big lovable idiot! *You* won't be able to see anything, either, and they say the trail's a sheer drop in places!"

He nodded and said, "If I can't see down a cliff it might not look as spooky. Staring over an edge at a mile-or-more drop can make one feel sort of tense, you know."

She moaned. "I feel sick just to think about such heights!"

He chuckled. "Me too. I mind a time I was cornered with my back to a considerable canyon, down in the Four Corners Country a while back. But I still got to get them more recent owlhoots and it ain't my fault they hid out such a dangerous place."

"Maybe I'd better come along and keep an eye on you," she ventured.

He laughed. "Not hardly. I mean it. I don't know why females keep insisting on tagging along where most *men* wouldn't want to go, if they had a lick of sense. But this is one time I don't aim to listen to sweet unreason, Wilma. I'll have enough on my plate without having to worry about a pretty gal plunging a mile in the dark!"

She shook her head wildly and said, "I was teasing. You'd never get me to go mountain climbing in the dark if my life depended on it! But what about *your* life, darling? Even if you manage not to walk off a cliff in the dark, the odds against you up there are still a dozen to one, and I thought we'd just established Custer shouldn't have tried that."

He said, "There's only half a dozen in the gang, and that's why they call my .44-40 a six-shooter. I'll have two extra rounds in my derringer, should it come to that. I'd like to take along my Winchester as well, but I may need both hands for getting over the rougher spots. So I'll leave it here with you. Don't use it on anyone unless he's ugly as well as forward, hear?"

She started to cry. Longarm growled, "Aw, mush," and got to his feet to put on his sheepskin and step outside.

The sky all around as well as above was black velvet spangled with more stars than usual at lower altitude. Some of the stars were moving, for at this height and time of the year one got to wish on a shooting star every few moments.

He couldn't see the summit or even a fair ways up from this hollow. But he knew which way it had to be. So he started up the gravel-strewn trail. As he came to a sort of saddle above the cabin he saw the ridges to the east were etched boldly against the blackness by a zig-zag line of lemon light. He knew the moon painting such a pretty picture couldn't be lagging too far behind its first rays.

He was right. By the time the trail was getting really steep and he'd made it to where Kincaid's diamond lay forted up among the rocks, the moon was peeking over the mountaintops at them like a big but sort of unripe pumpkin.

He'd just congratulated the dragoons on how smart they had their carbines trained when he heard hurried footsteps coming up the trail at them. He turned with a scowl to bawl Wilma out, then he saw it was the captain.

Kincaid bawled him out instead. The officer said, "This is dumb as hell, even for you. That girl reporter tells me you mean to go for the summit in the dark. I can't let you do that. It's just plain suicide."

"I hope you're wrong about that last part," Longarm said. "As to whether I need your permission or not, I got out of the army some time ago. That's how come I don't get to give *you* orders, neither."

Kincaid swore. "I don't want to fight about it, Long."

Longarm said, "Good. I got enough gents to fight, higher up. So that's where I'm headed."

Kincaid swore some more. "All right, you crazy bastard," he conceded. "I guess I'll just have to go with you and, if I fall over the edge, I'll never speak to you again."

Longarm shook his head and said, "Guess again, Matt. I was sent alone. You got a dragoon company to ride herd on down here and I'll be mad as hell if you let them bandits slip through you once they run away from me. I'm going up alone, to see if I can't convince them to give up, fight, or scatter. Like that old Arapaho told us that time, I have spoken."

Kincaid grimaced. "As I recall, **he died** shortly thereafter, too. You're going to wind up dead, pard."

Longarm shrugged. "I never figured on living for-ever. We can talk some more about it when I come back down. If I don't, we can't."

Then he turned away to trudge on and up. Kincaid considered ordering his men to try to stop him. But on reflection he knew he was responsible for their welfare, too, so he didn't.

Longarm moved out of sight around the bend. He stopped to take in the pretty moonlit scene, a wall of damp granite to his back and nothing to point his boot tips at but a pretty little moonlit lake, a hell of a ways down in a bowl of inky darkness.

Then he moved on. He saw he'd been right about the trail being easy enough to make out in the moonlight, even if he had been wrong about the drop-off to one side not being scary after dark. You didn't have to see bottom to sense it was down there, licking its stone chops like a big old black cat sniffing for mice. It didn't make him feel more secure when he trod on a loose pebble too small for the moon to shadow and too big to treat care-less. He sighed and said, "Why me, Lord. I've told you more than once I mean to give up cheroots and rye and sassy women one of these days. So let's cut down on this loose gravel, hear?"

The Lord didn't seem to be paying attention that night. A quarter of a mile on, a whole big slab of trail gave way as Longarm stepped on it, and he would have gone with it had not he flattened fast and dug all ten fingers into solid granite.

He lay there a moment, heart pounding against what

83

was left of the trail, and decided, "Anyone who got half a dozen ponies past here was crazy as well as lucky! Of course, this mountain may have been more solid before that last ferocious thunderstorm."

He rolled to a sitting position, hauled his boot heels back to solid ground, he hoped, and eased to his feet by sliding the back of his sheepskin up rough granite. Then he moved on.

As if to tempt him to further foolishness, the trail led him next to a stretch where the drop-off wasn't as sheer. Had he thought about it, he'd have known rolling down a mountain could hurt almost as much as just falling off it. But he was in a hurry and so, instead of thinking, he moved faster where it looked a mite safer.

But he still had to pause and consider each time he came to a hairpin, lest he stick his head around it into a gun muzzle. So after a time he became aware he was being followed up the trail.

That was a considerable improvement on footsteps *ahead* of him. He still drew his sixgun and moved into a cleft as he awaited the pleasure of whoever it might be.

As they came around a moonlit bend into view, hugging the high side, Longarm saw it was the Post Office men, Hamp and Gus. He holstered his gun and said, "Evening. Don't the moon look pretty, beaming down at us so bright?"

"What are *you* doing up here, Longarm?" Hamp asked. "I told you this was our case, damn it!"

Longarm smiled pleasantly. "I ain't greedy. Feel free to take the lead if you've a mind to. This trail ain't as solid as it looks in some places."

"We noticed," Gus said. "Was that you who kicked half the width of the path over the edge back there?"

"I didn't have to kick it loose. I'd say summer lightning must have done that earlier this afternoon. I thought you boys had already found this way up sort of discouraging."

Hamp said, "We did. It can't be helped. We just found out the Larimer County posse on the other side of this infernal mountain means to pull out any minute. So we got to get them rascals on the summit before they peer down at sunrise to see how disgusting this situation is."

Longarm nodded and said, "I'm glad to see the Postmaster General hires smarter gents than your average county sheriff."

Then Hamp proved him wrong by saying, "You're damned right. And you can't come along with us, Justice."

As the two edged past him, Longarm said, "I ain't coming along with you. I'm coming along with me."

They all moved on up the trail a ways before Hamp turned to yell, "God damn it, I told you this was *our* case!"

"Yell a little louder," Longarm said. "Sound carries well in these mountains, but we wouldn't want to take anyone by surprise. There's glory enough for everyone here, Hamp. I don't give a hang if you want credit for the arrest, as long as some damned somebody gets arrested. Them sons of bitches cleaned out the savings of a whole poor town. The fact they took the money from a post office safe is a tedious technicality we can argue about later."

"Longarm, we're just doing our job," Gus tried.

"What do you think *I'm* doing, climbing mountains as a *hobby?*" Longarm answered. "Go on ahead if you want to. Like I said, there's glory enough for everybody, and they still got us outgunned two to one."

That might have had a calming effect on their nerves. They didn't bother him any more as he followed them higher and higher. Gus, between Longarm and the surlier Hamp, even got friendly enough to warn Longarm, "Watch your step, Justice. We're close to the stretch they drove us back from. Big boulder ahead, as almost blocks the trail. This afternoon someone bounced a rifle round off it as we was trying to work our way past it."

The trail swung in to follow a steep hollow. Across the way, Longarm could make out the boulder Gus was talking about. He could see it had rolled down from above and then, cuss it, stuck on the trail instead of bouncing like a more considerate house-sized hunk of rock might have. Up ahead, Hamp called back, "It ain't light enough for such fancy shooting now."

Longarm raised his own voice just enough to carry the few yards between them. "Keep it down to a roar, damn it. Don't tell 'em we're coming. Let 'em guess!"

Hamp swaggered on, saying, "Go on back if you're scared."

Longarm *was* scared. Anyone with brains would have been. But he followed, anyway. Then, long before the loudmouth in the lead could get to the boulder ahead, someone behind it popped up to blaze away and Hamp was rolling ass over teakettle, yelling fit to bust. It wasn't clear whether he'd been gutshot or was just upset about dying so young. They couldn't see him when he hit, but the big, squishy thump seemed to quiet him considerable.

Chapter 7

By this time, of course, Longarm lay flat on the narrow trail, bouncing round after round off the top edge of that boulder. He heard someone yip like a kicked dog in the distance as, at the same time, boot heels ran over his prone form.

Longarm grunted, "Back my play. Gus!" as his gun ran dry. But Gus was long gone, so Longarm rolled to the meager cover of a cleft running up the high side and crouched in it to reload as he cussed old Gus and his family tree back to Adam and Eve.

But nobody fired on Longarm's position and as he calmed down he had to laugh. "Come to think on it, Gus, you may not be so dumb," he muttered. *"I* must be. I'm still here and you was right. There's just no way to work around that boulder up ahead."

Longarm rose to his feet in the rock chimney, risking his hat by holding it out invitingly. When nobody shot it from his grasp, he decided it might be safe to put it back on. He holstered his reloaded pistol as well. Then he braced his back against one side of the big crack, his boots against the other, and started inching up. He tried not to look down before he had to. When he did his heart skipped a beat. For while his common sense told him he would land on the narrow trail below, the ghastly depths seemed to be hoping he'd bounce. He muttered, "I wonder why some fools do this sort of thing when they don't have to."

He looked up again and still saw he couldn't work much higher, because the random cleft in the mountain didn't seem to go anywhere worth getting to. But from up so high he could see the far side of that boulder, now. Unless someone was hugging it closer, tight as a tick, the cuss with the rifle had run on up a ways. Longarm started back down the cleft he was wedged into. It was easier but just as frightening. He worked his way back to solid footing and ran up the trail for that boulder before someone else could get as foolhardy. He found he could work his way between the boulder and the high side. That sure beat going around it the spooky way. He dropped to one knee on the far side and struck a match. Sure enough, he scouted spent brass, .30-30, and what had to be blood. There wasn't much, just a ruby drop here and there. He nodded. "Good. I hit the bastard solid."

Then he stared thoughtfully at the boulder that had offered such temptations in the first place. "I don't know about you, rock. Unless you rolled down in that last big storm, I can't see how anyone got half a dozen ponies around you."

He got no answer from the mass of granite. The lichen growing here and there in patches on it didn't tell him much either. He shrugged and eased on up the trail. For, no matter how they'd made it past that boulder, they had, with at least one deer rifle.

Longarm knew his .44-40 revolver threw a more powerful round, less than a quarter as far. From time to time he spied little shiny red beads in the moonlight ahead. There were no footprints or even heel marks. None were to be expected on a trail cut in solid rock and peppered with frost-busted talus. He wondered who might have cut the trail in the first place, and why. He had read enough about the peak named after some distant relative to know there was no point in going up it. Like the hills all around, Long's Peak had been drilled for color by the first wild-eyed prospectors of the Colorado Gold Rush. They had found lots of rocks, interesting to a geologist, no doubt. But most of the core was solid granite and, while color was often found along the line where granite gave way to softer shales and sandstones plastered against it, Long's Peak had been a bust. Just a mighty big hunk of rock with a nice view, they said, from the top.

He couldn't see anyone going to this much trouble just so dudes could exclaim over scenery. Dudes did that a lot, for some reason. A serious trail like the one he was following had to have been left for a more serious reason. The trouble with survey maps was that they only showed where trails ran, and never said a word about who had left them. Longarm knew the transcontinental railroad had been partly built along old trails left by Indians and wild critters. He had seen nothing up here so far to tempt a deer with a whole Front Range to nibble on. Indians might have thought it was a spirit mountain. Long's Peak was said to be the highest bump in the Front Range.

Longarm wished more was known about the vanished Kimoho. Not because he wanted to convert to their religion, but because anyone taking a mountain that seriously might have run more than one trail up it. He knew the survey maps showed lesser trails, running partway and likely washed out in the higher parts by storms. The same map said this trail he was on led all the way to the top and that some parts of it were considered treacherous. It was nice to see that maps told the truth sometimes.

As he climbed around a scary hairpin he had more trouble seeing the way ahead. They had either cut the trail along here through darker shale, or something was wrong with the infernal moon.

He glanced over his shoulder and cursed. It was the moon. She was starting to act coy behind a cloud veil, and the damned old stars were gone entirely now.

He sat on a rock in a rocky niche to light a smoke as he pondered his next move. It didn't take as long to decide as it took to smoke down a cheroot. He swore, swore some more, and said aloud, "What the hell. Lightning can strike a fool going downhill just as hard as it can strike one going the other way."

He got up and moved on, cupping his smoke in one hand as he'd learned to do in the days drill sergeants yelled at him for smoking in ranks. Lots of good old boys on both sides had run out of luck because drill sergeants in Yankee blue or Confederate gray had spent more time lecturing growing boys about their disgusting habits than the finer points of staying alive.

Longarm had often wondered, since he'd taught himself, whether this had been because a good soldier and a kid who was interested in staying alive were a contradiction in terms. He knew he had likely been a better soldier, as his superiors saw a soldier, *before* he'd gotten good at ducking.

So an older and hopefully wiser Custis Long ducked behind a boulder, fast, when he sensed a blur of movement at the blurry limits of his vision ahead.

He watched and waited quite a spell, but nothing happened and he finally decided it had been a trick of the moonlight. There was enough of that to spare, now. For growly clouds were stampeding across the sky from the southwest in growing numbers and the mountains were starting to growl back as here and there a peak was outlined by a distant lightning strike.

Longarm moved faster along the narrow margin between life and death, not because he was dumb enough to expect much shelter up ahead, but because he hoped the sounds of the gathering storm might muffle an occasional crunch or the rattle of a rock he sent over the edge.

But as the moon was swallowed whole by a massive black thunderhead he had to stop, wedging his back in a cleft so the wind couldn't get between him and the high side, as he knew it would try to, in the swirling blackness closing in.

It was black as hell but still dry as the first bolt hit close enough to tingle every hair on Longarm's body as

93

it trimmed the weight of Long's Peak another mite. As he listened to the shattered rock coming down all around, Longarm had to allow the mountain could spare a hundred pounds or so better than he could. He tried to work deeper into the same as he muttered, "All right, Rock of Ages, cleft for me. Open up and let me hide myself in thee, even if it ain't the Sabbath."

But then the rain commenced to come down by the washtubs and the next thing he knew a roaring whitewater creek seemed to be using his cleft as a vertical bed. That no doubt explained how the shallow cleft had gotten there in the first place. He got out of it before the rapidly gathering force could wash him away to certain doom. He still felt doomed as he crouched a few yards farther up the mountain with his soggy back to the rocks while the wind and the rain tried to teach him to fly.

Another bolt sizzled in to make both Longarm and the solid rock shudder. "This ain't fair, Lord," he growled. "If you really mean to cut down on sinners, it was them sons of bitches up the mountain, not me, as robbed that post office in Jimtown!"

Most of the bolts were, in fact, striking higher up, illuminating the rocks around him for split seconds. Longarm started crawling up the trail, rubbing the soggy left shoulder of his sheepskin on wet rock as if he'd been a worried cat hugging the security of the baseboarding in a strange house. It reminded him of times he'd been under artillery fire in the dark. It reminded him how often he'd sworn that he never meant to do it again, once this infernal war was over.

As he groped his way along he seemed to be losing

the security of high rock to his left. It still rose to that side, albeit not as steeply. He didn't want to think about what might be going on to his right. Then lightning lit up his path as if to show him the way, and in the all-too-short moment of vision he'd seen the trail was swinging inward, away from the sheer side of the mountain, where some forgotten trailblazer, bless his hide, had found a steeper but less treacherous route toward the summit.

He still stayed on his hands and knees as he continued to climb, for when the trail winding up the steep slope was not in use as a fair-weather path it seemed to think it was a mountain brook. The water rushing over his wrists and into his boots was cold as ice. The rain was much warmer. He knew he was catching snow-melt as well. But, looking on the sunny side as he crawled through the howling blackness, he figured that could mean he was getting a mite closer to the summit. It had to be *somewhere* up yonder. He'd been aboard this fool mountain an eternity.

The route he was following now seemed just about right for a mountain goat, but hardly fit for ponies. That could be read two ways: the bandits had been riding mountain goats, or they'd dismounted farther down and somehow nobody had noticed.

He'd not had a chance to jaw with or, hell, even *see* but a small part of the combined posse wrapped around the lower slopes. It was possible stray mounts had been spotted or even rounded up on the far side. If so, that would be considerable help once the owlhoots noticed they weren't boxed in so good after all. A gang on foot would have a time getting far enough to matter if even some of the law was left up here by sunrise. He sincerely hoped the sons of bitches were as wet and miserable as everyone else by now. Caves were rare in rock like the rock all around, and the notion of yet another abandoned cabin seemed silly.

He'd just told himself that when he crawled around a pile of house-sized boulders to see a light in a window ahead.

He stared soberly at the small square of lamplight shining through what looked like oiled parchment or mighty dirty glass as he muttered, "Aw, shit. They're forted up warm and dry. But at least we know now why they headed for such an unlikely place. For if they provisioned ahead, they're fixed to hold out through a whole winter, and we've already lost most of our posse riders."

He could see well enough now to move the rest of the way up on his feet. So he rose, drew his .44-40, and did so. Ordering six men out into a thunderstorm would have sounded dumb even had they wanted to obey him. There was just no way he was going to disarm and herd that many prisoners in this ink shower. Had it not been so nasty out, he'd have considered waiting till sunrise before making his play. But he doubted it was midnight yet and he knew he was already dangerously chilled at an altitude where even healthy lungs had trouble keeping a body going.

He decided, what the hell, they had the advantage of knowing where everyone inside was, while he had the advantage of surprise. He unhooked his derringer from his watch chain and held that in his left hand as he advanced with his more serious gun trained on the one door in or out. If he could kick it in with his first try, he'd have a good chance at getting the drop on them.

Should the damned door hold, he'd be in a whole lot of trouble. He made up his mind to kick like hell.

But he still had a good twenty yards to go when the door popped open. Longarm almost fired at the figure in the doorway before he decided a female outlined so curvily by lamplight had to be a most unlikely post office robbery suspect.

Lefty Page could have described the owlhoots he'd seen sort of fuzzy, however, so Longarm kept his guns trained on her as she called out, "Who's there? Is that you and the doctor, Sis?"

He called back, "No, ma'am. I'm the law. Deputy U.S. Marshal Long, and if I'm confusing you, you're confounding me even more. You folk sure picked an unlikely quarter-section to homestead, no offense. We have to be more'n two miles above sea level, more like three, and nobody mentioned human beings living up here on Long's Peak."

She said, "I'm Feather Garson. You must be soaking wet. Come in. Do you know anything about gunshot wounds, sir?"

He kept his voice polite as he said he might. He kept his guns handy as he followed her inside. The walls all around were made of free-stone. A warm but thrifty fire on the hearth across the way had everything but him snug and dry. Up close he could see his hostess was a handsome little breed of eighteen or so, dressed in cheap red calico that still went nicely with her dusky skin, braided jet-black hair and big sloe eyes. A white man of sixty or more was wrapped in a Hudson Bay blanket on the stone floor near the fireplace. His eyes were closed. His silvery head was wrapped in white linen, stained with four bits' worth of blood.

The girl said, "My sister left to find a doctor some time ago. I'm so worried about Pappy. He hasn't stirred for at least an hour."

Longarm felt it was safe to put his guns away in a one-room cabin occupied by one young gal and a dead man. He knew that waxy look, starting at the nose, but it was considered common courtesy to go through the motions.

He hunkered down by the old man, setting his own soggy hat aside to dry on the hearth as he felt the base of the dead man's neck. Such warmth as was left in the flesh could be accounted for by the nearby fire.

Longarm stared soberly up at the worried-looking girl and murmured gently, "I fear your father is beyond medical attention, Miss Feather."

She gasped and sobbed, "Oh, no, he can't be dead, not Pappy!"

"How do you reckon he wound up with that bullet in his head?" Longarm asked.

She fell to her knees on the hearth to cradle the dead man's head in her lap as she commenced to keen in the Indian fashion.

Longarm saw no need to press her in her time of grief. He rose to peel off as much of his wetness as he felt decent. As he stood with his back to the fire to at least warm up his wet pants and shirt he studied the modest furnishings of the cabin. There were sleeping platforms at one end, taking advantage of the way heat rises. There were boxes, barrels, and tools along the walls, but no tables or chairs. They'd been living more like Indians than whites, eating off the floor, seated around the fire, most likely. There was an old cast-iron spider and some clay baking pots closer to the massive fireplace. The scene read best as an old squaw man living alone of late with the results of his union.

He lit a smoke and when he spied a brown bottle on a nearby black-powder barrel he helped himself. The keening gal at his feet seemed in no mood to offer or be asked. It was trade liquor. He'd tasted worse, and at least it helped his teeth stop chattering. He had just re-corked the bottle and put it back when the door burst open and a soaking wet bear came in, sobbing, "It's no use! The trail's turned into a roaring river! How's Pappy, and . . . Oh!"

Longarm nodded and said, "I'm Deputy U.S. Marshall Custis Long, ma'am. As you might surmise from the way your kid sister's crying, your efforts would have been in vain in any case."

As she shucked out of her buffalo robe and wool head scarves to let them fall wherever they had a mind to, Longarm saw she was bigger and stronger-looking as well as a year or so older than the keening one. Her calico dress was blue. It was clinging to her more vo-luptuous curves as see-through as thin wet cloth could. But, as if she hated to make a strange man guess about any details, she calmly stripped her wet dress off over her head and moved to join her sister, naked as a jay.

Longarm knew this was hardly the time to consider such matters, but he had to admit she was as pretty as her kid sister after all, now that he could see her better.

She pulled Feather away from the corpse and held her in a big-sisterly embrace, soothing, "There, there, we knew he was done for before I left. He wouldn't want you keening on like this, Feather. Pappy was a man, not a crybaby."

Feather sobbed, "Oh, Star, whatever will become of us now?"

It was a good question. To answer it, Longarm had to know more. Star had just shown she tended to take a practical approach to disaster. So he asked her, "Do you ladies consider yourselves Indian or otherwise?"

"Pappy was English. Mammy was Kimoho. What difference does that make now?" Star said.

"That's up to you ladies," he said. "English-speaking breeds is allowed to live as white as they want to act. On the other hand, if need be, you could throw yourselves on Uncle Sam's blanket if you feel the need to be looked after as orphaned Ho."

She grimaced and said, "That'll be the day. Pappy always said we might outlive him. So he raised us to take care of ourselves when the time came, and I guess it has. We got money in the bank down in Ward. We ain't had much schooling, but Pappy taught us how to read and write and warned us about some of the ways his own kind tries to slicker Kimoho gals."

Longarm nodded soberly. "I reckon he would have

knowed about such matters. Can we talk about who gunned him, now?"

Star nodded grimly. "It was outlaws. Feather and me was here in the cabin, so we didn't see it. Pappy was worried about strangers on his mountain. It's been getting sort of crowded lately. This evening after supper he went out to see if they was still about. He'd traded shots with 'em earlier. A while later he come staggering home, shot in the head. Don't ask me how. Pappy was always a mighty tough man. He wasn't able to make much sense. He mumbled something about a dirty trick, then he passed out. The rest you know."

Longarm shook his head. "Not by half, Miss Star. To begin with, I come up this way with a mess of other lawmen after a gang of owlhoots. We've been getting shot at sort of tedious. Is it possible we have us a serious if honest mistake here?"

Both gals gasped in horror, but the calmer Star decided, "No. Pappy knew there was lawmen and even some soldiers spread out down below. He mentioned it to us last night, as a matter of fact. He said they could be after some *others* he suspected might be up here and warned us to stay close to the cabin till the matter got sorted out."

Feather raised her tear-streaked face from her sister's naked breast and added, "Pappy was never no outlaw, damn it!"

Longarm nodded. "That's another thing I'd like to know more about. No offense, but I'll be whipped with snakes if I can see how anyone could make an honest living this far up a bald mountain. What do you all raise on this steep, rocky slope, eagle eggs?"

"Pappy was a mining man," Star explained. "Not up here. He just *liked* it up here, where a man could feel free and no nosy neighbors could talk about us because our mother was Kimoho. When we needed provisions he'd go down to the sissier parts of the world."

"On foot?"

"Well, sure. The trails are too tricky for horses, even if you could keep horses up here. He generally hiked down to Ward or sometimes as far as Lyons if he wanted to pack something serious back up."

"Pappy had strong legs," Feather explained.

Longarm said, "He'd have to, packing provisions a dozen miles or more uphill. Let's get back to how he might have *paid* for even modest provisions, ladies. We just agreed this eagle's nest he chose to live in can't be a money-making proposition."

Feather said, "That's easy. We told you he was a mining man. He worked here and about down below as need be. Even panned tailings left by more careless folk. Pappy had took a course in mining before coming west and he often said it was a caution how much color a sloppy mining operation just threw away."

Longarm knew that was true. He'd once met a teacher and his wife, camped near Pikes Peak for the summer vacation, who said they made a modest profit working abandoned try-holes for crumbs of missed gold. Men running a mine as a business with a payroll to meet couldn't take the time to sniff out every tiny bit of color. They knew it was there. They just didn't care.

Lots of eccentric loners worked piles of tailings and even the ashes of abandoned and burnt stamp mills for a modest profit. Half an ounce of gold added up to more than a cowhand made in a week, and nobody got to yell at you as you poked about with your own pan.

He said, "Well, far be it from me to tell ladies with a bank account in Ward where they'll want to be staying or not staying. I know this may seem indelicate, but I still think it might be a good notion to move your father farther away from that fire. It ain't doing him a bit of good, and he'll keep better if we let him cool, some."

Feather started to cry again. The more practical Star gently pushed back on her haunches and said, "I'll carry his feet if you'll grab his shoulders. We can leave him in the lean-to out back for now."

Longarm thought that was a sensible notion, so they picked the corpse up and carried him out into the rain. Star took the lead and they got him feet first to the uphill side, where, sure enough, a sloping plank structure, half filled with supplies, had been thrown up against the blank stone wall. As they carried the dead man in Star suggested stretching him out atop some crates.

Longarm said, "Not if you keep food in them crates, ma'am."

"Oh, you're right, we'd best lay him here on the dirt. How long do you think we have to bury him? I'm not used to dealing with dead folk, but a deer can sure get rank in a day or so."

As they stretched the blanket-wrapped cadaver in as dignified a position as they could manage, bending him a mite around a nail keg, Longarm said, "You'll have a day or so to get him down to the nearest churchyard, Miss Star."

She straightened up, her wet naked breasts almost brushing Longarm's wet shirt front, and told him, "Pappy didn't hold much with the Jesus notion. Said Mammy's religion was silly, too. I know a nice place to leave him, once the rain stops and things sort of simmer down. There's this hollow lookout, farther up the mountain. Pappy used to set up there for hours in fine weather, just staring, like he owned everything he could see from up there. I think he'd like to be left there. Under some rocks, of course."

Longarm sensed she was about to break down. He already had one keening squaw to deal with. He took her gently in his arms and told her, "I think that's a grand notion, Miss Star. I'm sure your father's four spirits will feel proud and free up yonder."

He'd meant to hug her, brotherly. It wasn't easy when a strange wet naked lady was built so nice. She didn't help his platonic concern when she snuggled closer to calmly say, "I want to do Pappy proud. We was mighty fond of each other."

"He said, "Maybe we'd best go back in the cabin, now." "Yeah, it's cold out here," she said. "You'll be staying the night with us anyway, right?"

As she took his hand to lead him back to shelter he said, "I can't see floundering about in this storm. You said something about a trail being flooded out. Were you talking about the steep side, Miss Star?"

She said, "No. That way's quicker but dangerous. I

headed down the other side, where it's windy as hell but less apt to kill you after dark. Nobody but a real fool would try the cliffside trail after sundown."

"I noticed. My point is that the map don't show but the one trail, Miss Star."

She shrugged her bare shoulders and replied, "I doubt this cabin and a lot of things I know have been put down on charting paper. Me and Feather was half-riz on this mountain. We know it like we know our own bodies. Maybe better. There are times a woman's body can surprise her. Are you feeling snuggly? I don't know why on earth I should be at a time like this, but like I said, life is filled with surprises."

He said, "Let's talk about them owlhoots your father was worried about with all-too-good reasons. Lord knows where he run into them. But I still suspicion it had to be still higher up. Come sunrise, could you put me on a good trail to the crest, mayhaps one we don't have charted?"

They opened the door and ducked inside. "Sure," she said, "I know a couple of ways to the top. Guess what, Sis? He's willing to stay the night with us!"

Feather gasped and started bawling again. Longarm said, "The reason I need your help are as follows. I can't see anyone on a pony taking the official trail I took. Unless they *legged* her to the top, for whatever reason, they know this mountain a lot better than we suspected and, come the cold cruel dawn, they'll be able to see many a gap in our lines below. I'll want you ladies to study the view as well, and offer me some educated guesses as to their best bust-out route. Do you think it's remotely possible a man could ride a horse down the gentler slopes, sudden?"

"If he didn't worry about his neck too much," Star said. "I've never seen a horse near the crest and I've lived up here quite a spell. But, yeah, I think it could be done, by one hell of a rider on one hell of a horse. It would still be a mighty long dash across the much wider apron slopes to timberline, though."

He said, "I know. But we've established 'em as reckless old boys and, with not too many down there to stop 'em, they'd have a better than even chance. On the other hand, they may mean to stay forted up on the crest a spell. How do you feel about that?"

She shrugged her bare shoulders, making her perky brown breasts bounce. *"We've* stayed up here many a winter. It depends on how much provision they have with 'em. There's still plenty of warm days left to build rock shelters, and Lord knows enough *rocks* up yonder to build with."

Longarm grimaced and said, "I wish you hadn't said that. I'd best go on up in the morning and make sure they don't do that."

She nodded. "We'd best bed down, then."

Chapter 8

The horrendous storm blew over before dawn and the sudden silence woke Longarm better than an alarm clock could have. The two sisters were already awake.

They ate a quick meal of ham and eggs, and it was still fair dark as the three of them headed up a trail he would have never found by himself. Star was armed with a ten-gauge. Feather packed an old muzzle-loading English Parker they said was a family heirloom. When he asked which one their late father had favored most Feather said, "He had his own repeating rifle. I sure hope we find it where he dropped it, soon. Guns rust awful up here if you don't keep 'em oiled and under cover most of the time."

He didn't answer. He still hoped he could be wrong.

The sun was just rising when Star stopped them in a hollowed-out flat spot to say, "This is where we'll be leaving Pappy."

Longarm gazed out over a hundred miles or more of glorious sunrise-painted view and said soberly, "By God, ladies, if this ain't a fit tomb for a pharaoh, they'd play hell finding him a better one!"

Feather asked what a pharaoh was. He said, "Ancient kings of Egypt land."

Star said, "That sounds like Pappy. He was king of this mountain."

As she led him farther toward the crest Longarm said, "I've been wondering when you all moved up here?"

"Shortly before Mammy died. We used to live on Trapper's Rock, another high point as wasn't quite this private. Folk around Ward got to talking mean about us, even though we wasn't doing anything mean to them. Pappy said it was because we was part Kimoho. So we moved up here when I was about ten and Sis, here, was seven or eight."

"I got a reason for asking these questions. By any chance, do either of you ladies know of any visitors your Pappy had up here?"

Star thought for a moment. "Some. From time to time Pappy brought company home. Not often."

"Do you recall any names?" Longarm went on.

She laughed. "Like I said, it's been a spell. For some reason Pappy didn't have too many friends down around Ward."

Feather asked, "What about that one Pappy called Lefty, Sis?"

Before Star could answer Longarm asked, "Lefty Page? Tall as me but leaner, keeps a black silk bandanna tight around his neck?"

"That sounds like him," Star said. "I remember the

bandanna. I think he said he raises horses. I like him. Do you know him, Custis?"

"You say him and your father had some sort of business together, Star?"

Feather said, "I can answer that. Pappy sometimes hired horses off that gent. I heard 'em talking about it."

"When he come up here with your father, were they walking or riding? Think hard. It could be important," Longarm said.

They both said "Walking" at the same time. Feather added, "I remember Lefty telling Pappy he could see, now, why he didn't keep his own remuda. Pappy told him it was just as well, since they both made money on the deal."

"What deal was that, Feather?"

"Gee, I don't know. Pappy hardly ever took us down from this mountain with him. He said he didn't like folk gossiping about our Kimoho blood. Anyhow, he left us up here, and sometimes it got lonesome as hell."

Star stopped and pointed at a rise ahead that looked much like all the others they'd been over, so far. "That's it," she said. "This mountain don't get no higher, Custis."

He nodded, drew his revolver, and, while he was at it, asked if he could borrow her ten-gauge. When she handed it to him he said, "Stay here. If you hear gunshots run back down to the cabin and bar the door. I'm going the rest of the way alone."

He did. The grade was steeper than it looked, but after a time he was king of the mountain and the view was fantastic. But he was alone up there. He could see the two girls below him as red and blue dots. He couldn't tell if anyone was there or not, way down, until the sun caught a flapping army guidon right and told him Kincaid's dragoons, at least, were still acting like men. To one side, between him and the girls, a sizeable patch of snow remained unmelted in a hollow. He poked about until he found a hollow more exposed to the summer sun and moved down to scout it.

There wasn't much sign. All he found was a corroded spent shell, .30-30. He picked up the blackened bit of brass and worked his way around and down to rejoin the girls. He returned the shotgun and asked, "Would that rifle your father went out with have been a .30-30 deer hunter?"

Star said, "It surely was. Don't tell us you found it."

He didn't. He doubted either would ever speak to him again if they put it together the way he'd just had to. He didn't know why he'd had to shoot it out with their father. He just knew that was the only answer.

They had all been slickered. The damned post-office robbers had never come up here in the first place! He said, "I found an old deer-brass your father must have left, chasing eagles off his mountain a spell back. Them others we both seem to have been worried about seem to have slipped away in the dark after all. I'd be obliged if you ladies would direct me to the quickest way down, now."

Star said, "Well, the cliff side is the quickest and it's broad day, now."

110

"Oh, that one's so scary, Sis," Feather protested.

Longarm said, "I noticed. It still puts me back at that other cabin, sudden. So how do I find the top end of it?"

Star pointed. "That way. We want to go with you."

Longarm said, "No. You've still got to do something decent about your father's remains, and I haven't time to wait for you to pack. I left a horse down below. Everyone else will be riding out, too. If you're worried about that bank in Ward, I'll put in a good word for you there before I have to head back to Denver. Which one is it?"

Star said, "There's only one. Ward ain't much bigger than Jimtown. But can't you wait for us? Folk down in Ward always treat us mean. It ain't our fault we're part Kimoho, is it?"

"I'm sorry," Longarm said. "And I thank you for your help. I'm sure you two pretty gals will make your way in the world just fine. Now, I still got some criminals to chase, and it's getting late."

Then he turned and headed down the mountain.

Kincaid's dragoons spotted Longarm before he got to the lower cabin, and sent word ahead. As Longarm strugged the last weary steps Wilma Wadsworth tore out of the cabin to greet him, with the young officer trailing at a slower pace.

Wilma wrapped her arms around Longarm and sobbed, "Oh, we've been so worried about you, Custis! We heard that Postal Inspector was hurt. Where have you been all this time?"

"Old Hamp wasn't hurt. He was killed. Did his partner ever stop running?" Longarm asked.

Matt Kincaid joined them to say, "I can answer that. Gus Polk rode back down with Under-Sheriff Love's men. I tried to hold them here, but once they heard Grand and Larimer Counties had pulled out, there was no stopping them. Since you're still alive after all this time, is it safe to assume you got the rascal who got Hamp Hampshire?"

Aware that a newspaper reporter was hugging him, however sweet on him she might be, Longarm said, "You can write him off as hit and assumed dead, for now. We can talk about it off the record and as one man to another, later. I already told your men up the trail the war was over. They still think it's up to you to pull 'em in. You got 'em trained good, Matt."

"Not good enough to surround a whole mountain enough to matter," Kincaid said. "What do you mean about it being over?"

"Just what I said. We was slickered. They never went up there to begin with. In the first place, they couldn't have, on ponies. In the second place, I've been all the way to the top and back without spotting sign."

"Couldn't they have slipped down another way? It's a mighty big mountain, and we've had it surrounded mighty thin."

Longarm shook his head and said, "It won't work. You may have noticed it was mighty inclement last night. Even Eskimo would have had to build a fire to get through such a night in the open. Nobody built no fire, save for where I was, so nobody spent the night up yonder. I failed to spot so much as a cigar butt, and a half-dozen men always leave more sign than that."

"You must have frozen, even with a fire, poor thing?" Wilma asked.

He looked away and muttered, "Oh, I was in what you might call a rock shelter, so I was warm enough to get by."

Then, to change the subject, he told Kincaid, "We left Miss Wilma's sidesaddle farther down, without no horse. Would you have a mount to lend her at least as far down as the Middle Fork, Matt?"

Kincaid said, "Sure. We can let her use one of our pack brutes, going downhill with less to pack, now. I don't understand all this at all, pard. How did we all wind up up here if it was all just a snipe hunt?"

Longarm said, "I've been wondering about that for some time now. Neither you, me, them post office men, nor even the other posse riders from all over creation ever *tracked* any wild geese this far out of Jimtown, Matt. We was all responding to the loud cries for help from that *first* fool posse!"

Kincaid scowled. "I'd choose a better word than 'fool' if I wasn't in mixed company. Come to think of it, Under-Sheriff Love yanked Whitey Jung's badge for incompetence and chased him off this mountain *before* you found out we'd all been given a bum steer. It's sure a poser. But come on inside and wrap yourself around some breakfast while I gather my own men in."

Longarm shook his head. "I already ate. I'm depending on you to get Miss Wilma, here, back down to civilization. Old Strawberry and me will be riding on, now."

Wilma gasped, "Oh, no!"

Kincaid asked him what his hurry could be, adding, "It's not as if any of us have better places to go than back now, you know. The game's over. Those outlaws could be most anywhere now, with a good four days' lead and any sign they might have left, going anywhere, rained on as well!"

Longarm said, "They still have to be somewhere, and the money they rode off with was the rightsome property of poor folk. I know Love fired Jung for acting dumb. Love never struck me as a genius neither. So, for openers, I mean to see if I can find out how Jung managed to feel so sure he was tracking that gang to where they never went."

Kincaid nodded. "Some of my men are fair trackers. If we all ride back together, scouting sharp—"

But Longarm cut in with, "Jung never said he tracked anybody up the easy Skull Trail. He said the owlhoots took the Dead Cow Creek Trail. Your map shows 'em joining as one, just below timberline. I think I remember passing a sort of deer path about where the trees was starting to thin out. If that ain't the junction, I'll ride about a bit until I find that other trail. Then I mean to backtrack it all the way back to the wagon trace between Ward and Jimtown. It hardly seems possible Jung and his first posse could have followed a trail that long without spotting sign at all."

"Maybe," Kincaid said. "I don't envy you the task of

telling outlaw sign from posse sign. The posse was way bigger, and . . . have you considered the less charitable way to put all this together?"

Longarm nodded grimly. "From the first moment I began to suspect I was climbing the wrong mountain. Like Wilma here says, good old boys get clannish and, sure, Whitey could have been out to throw everyone off the trail of his pals by leading everyone the wrong way. But that would make him so dumb I doubt he could think up a ruse like that."

"Why would it be dumb?" asked Wilma. "It seems to me a lawman in league with bandits would *want* to lead everyone else on a wild-goose chase."

Kincaid was smart enough to tell her, "He's right. After leading the first hot pursuit the wrong way it would have been awfuly stupid of a crook leading a posse of inexperienced lawmen to call on *professionals* for assistance. Jung didn't have to. He could have just let his enthusiastic cowhands ride about up here until they decided they'd somehow lost the scent, and that would have been that. But he yelled for help, loud, and that's why we all know, sooner than anyone might have, that whichever way those bandits went, it couldn't have been *this* way."

She brightened. "Oh, I see. If you hadn't arrived with so many soldiers, and Under-Sheriff Love hadn't ridden up with a bigger posse, it might have seemed more believable that those six men had somehow slipped away. And if that poor Mr. Hampshire hadn't insisted on pressing up the mountain, and if Custis, here, hadn't insisted on pressing all the way to the top, everyone might still be barking up the wrong mountain?"

"Close enough," Longarm said. "I got to get on down to Dead Cow Creek Trail and read me some sign, now."

Chapter 9

It wasn't easy. Finding the spot where the other trail joined Skull Trail below timberline was no problem. After that it was mostly downhill in more than one sense. The trail the owlhoots were supposed to have followed seemed at first glance to be, if anything, the better route to Long's Peak from Jimtown. The footing was solid and everyone agreed the far end was closer to the scene of the robbery by a mile or more. But after they had worked down through broody spruce to the lower-growing aspen, Longarm could see why Lefty Page had advised him to follow Skull Trail. The aspen had been thick enough coming up *that* way. This was worse.

The only good thing to be said for pushing a posse through so much spinach was that it left plenty of sign. The trail was too narrow in places for one rider to punch through without scraping some. So there were stirrup blazes, fresh ones, on many a pale tree trunk, where a rider had torn the soft aspen bark down to bare white wood with his hung-up stirrup and no doubt some cussing.

117

The horrendous storms since the last time anyone else had been over this trail had washed out any clear hoofprints anyone on either side might have left. So when they got to how the trail got its name, Longarm reined in and dismounted.

The reasonably dry trail they had backtracked this far left the banks of the creek at an angle. From there on down it followed the creek, or tried to. The narrow strip of bare soil was more dimpled mud than solid dirt, edged on the high side with a knee-high growth of skunk cabbage and death camus where alder didn't bully its way almost into the creek. A lot of alder stems had been busted and trampled into the mud. No doubt half the riders had ridden around through the water. Dead Cow Creek was prettier than its surroundings. The bottom was fairly flat and gravel-paved. The water rippling over it was no more than a foot deep, maybe less, when it hadn't been raining so much.

Longarm told Strawberry, "Anyone knows, now, that nobody too important rode for Long's Peak, no matter what that posse thought. Let's see where one can get to, following the creek itself farther up. I can see there's no *path* following her. But all that water has to come from some damn wheres."

Strawberry didn't want to go. The water was freezing cold and the gravel underfoot was mossy and slick as butter. He led her upstream anyway, squishing his wet socks in water-filled boots.

The creek commenced to narrow and deepen as it was forced to run between boulders now and again.

Longarm decided the upper reaches would make a nice trout stream, if only there was a better way to reach it. They punched through a stretch where it was wider and hemmed in by a solid hedge of alder on either side. As they rounded a bend he spotted black and white patches on what seemed at first another boulder along the far edge. But boulders hardly ever grew hair and a black tail swishing in the running water. So, knowing dead horseflesh spooked live horses, Longarm tethered Strawberry to a stouter-looking alder trunk and moved on up for a closer inspection.

Lefty Page had said one of the gang rode past him on a paint. He'd been right about her being unshod, too. Saddle and bridle had been taken. The cause of death was easy to read. Someone had placed a gun muzzle against the white blaze just above the poor brute's left eye.

Longarm bent to lift each submerged leg in turn before he told the dead pony, "Unless you was stove-in more unusual I'd say you was just plain murdered, Paint. I'd sure like to know why."

He recovered his own mount and led her past the big corpse along the far side. Strawberry still rolled her eyes and argued with him a mite until the dead pony was out of sight. Then Longarm cursed when he saw he'd have to do that all over again, for they had come to a waterfall.

It wasn't high enough for a landscape painter to be interested in, but it was too steep for further wading, and the rock ledge it plunged over didn't offer easy climbing.

Longarm tied Strawberry up and climbed it anyway. But as he got his head above the treacherous, mossy rim he saw that he had wasted considerable effort, for he was staring at an even higher cliff and the birthplace of Dead Cow Creek. The water gushed out of cracks in the sheer rocks above. He swore and lowered himself back down.

As he fought Strawberry past the dead pony again he told her, "The notion that they found themselves boxed and shot their mounts to go on afoot was dumb to begin with. There were at least six of 'em, remember?"

Strawberry didn't answer, but his voice had a calming effect on her. The rest of the way down Dead Cow Creek Trail was just a muddy pain in the ass. When they finally busted out to where the creek crossed the wagon trace between Ward and Jimtown he patted Strawberry's neck. "There you go. You for some oats and me for dry socks," he said.

As they rode into the quiet hamlet he saw a new paper sign in the window of the general store. It read that they were going out of business and offered half-price on everything. There didn't seem to be a mad stampede to take advantage of such bargains. A kid in army blue was sitting on the steps, whittling. Longarm waited until he had dismounted and tethered Strawberry to the hitch rail out front before he asked the dragoon how come, saying, "I thought by now you boys would have made it halfway back to your garrison."

"So did we," the dragoon said. "It ain't fair. The Postmaster General's put Captain Kincaid in charge up here till they can send a team of smarter inspectors."

Longarm nodded and said, "I didn't think much of the first two. Is the captain out back?"

The dragoon shook his head. "That wasn't fair, neither. They asked us to recover the body of that gent of theirn as fell off the mountain. The army recovers its own dead. Why can't the damned old Post Office?"

"Maybe they're short-handed. You mean poor Kincaid had to go all the way back to Long's Peak?"

"He didn't sound like he liked it, neither. He left most of us here. He ain't a bad sort for an officer. Told us to expect him back by sundown and meanwhile to guard this post office. So that's what I'm doing. Guarding it. It's all right if you want to shop in the general store, though. It's just the post office as is closed until further notice."

Longarm nodded. "Much obliged. I sure need dry socks. Would you happen to know whatever happened to that reporter gal, Miss Wadsworth?"

The young soldier nodded and said, "Sure I would. We swung outten our way so's she could pick up a mount of her own at some old ranch. When we got here, and you wasn't here, the captain said you'd likely gone on back to Denver. That's when she lit out. The captain seemed to find that sort of amusing. That was before he got the wire from the Postmaster General, of course."

Longarm thanked the kid and went inside. He found Polly Clark behind her counter, looking sort of lost and lonely. He said, "Morning, ma'am. I used up all the socks I brought along with me. Can you fix me up with some?"

She said she could and asked his size. When he told

her, she refused to believe him and made him test her notion that he had to have smaller feet than that by wrapping a sock around his clenched fist and saying, "You are a big one, aren't you?"

He didn't see any need to argue. He'd always been big for his age. He said two pairs for a quarter sounded fair and asked her how come she was holding a sale.

She brushed a strand of hair from her brow with a weary hand. "I have to get rid of all this stock at any price. I've been put out of business," she told him.

He frowned and asked who would do such a mean thing to such a sweet little widow woman. "The Postmaster General," she said. "I just lost my appointment. I think they're going to make the blacksmith the new postmaster here."

"Don't you think they're being a little hard on you, ma'am?"

She sighed and said, "Tell *them* that. I don't think it was my fault we got robbed, either. But apparently I bent some of the rules about running a post office and they were out to shift some of the blame."

As she started to wrap his new socks he took them from her to just shove in a side pocket. "No sense wasting paper. You say they hung it on you, Miss Polly? How do they figure you was lax?"

She shrugged. "Exceeding my authority and not keeping proper records, according to that mean Inspector Hampshire who questioned me yesterday. He said I had no call to use the post office safe as a bank. I told him I wasn't banking, I was simply letting customers use the only safe in town. He said the post office isn't supposed to do that. Only funds for stamps, money orders, and such was to be kept in government premises. When I told him I owned the whole infernal building he got all red in the face and actually cussed in front of me. The nicer one, Inspector Polk, said he'd like to see my carbons of the receipts I'd given folk for money I let them store in my safe. When I said I wasn't one for paperwork he got sort of mad, too, although he was too well-brought-up to cuss me."

"I noticed he acted sort of sissy, ma'am," Longarm said. "Ain't it usual to give someone some sort of paper proof when they hand you money they might want back some day?"

She said, "I've been over all that with the sheriff's department. As I told them, I trust most of my customers and they trust me. I'm not stupid. I can remember when someone gives me an envelope or a money bag to keep for them. I did give 'em IOU notes. I did make everyone put their names on the packages they gave me. So all anyone had to do when someone asked for something back was to reach in the safe and get it out for them. Does that sound stupid?"

"Yes, ma'am," Longarm said, "no offense. Without official records, how is anyone to ever prove what they might or might not have lost to the bandits?"

"Under-Sheriff Love was interested in that, too. But in the end he had to allow it was no big deal. Whatever anyone says they left in my safekeeping, those robbers *got* it all. The county asked if any of it had been insured by anyone and, when I told them not to be silly, Under-Sheriff Love opined that since the money was likely gone forever, round numbers from memory was no worse than exact figures. I sure wish the Postmaster

General understood how folks do business out here. How's a body to run a general store and fill out all those silly papers they send us to fill out?"

He said, "They've been making me fill things out in triple doses since Grant got diselected, too. I take it the books you keep on groceries, hardware, and such show more red than black?"

She looked blank. He said, "Never mind. Stupid question. In sum, you don't make enough on this store operation alone to stay afloat. So without the stipend from the Postal Department you're selling out?"

She nodded. "It's been bad enough, just getting by, selling stamps as well as socks. I confess I've never had a head for business. My late husband kept the books when he was alive and he tried to teach me how. But it's not as if running a little crossroads operation in such a small place keeps one busy enough to write everything down. I've got a cigar box full of notepaper and old envelopes somewhere about. Some folks asking for credit tend to forget what they owe you if they suspect you might not know. So, sure, I made a note when I let someone have a sack of flour on the someday. There's no sense writing down a cash sale like I just made, is there?"

He smiled down at her. "I reckon not. I saw you put that quarter in your till. I got to haul on my new socks and get something inside me now. I don't suppose you'd know if the saloon here in Jimtown serves a decent noonday dinner?"

"Heavens, I didn't know it was getting that late," she said. "I don't know anything about the cooking at the

124

saloon, if they cook anything at all. But I can feed you while I'm feeding me, if you don't mind home cooking."

He chuckled. "I like everything sort of homey, ma'am. You'll have to let me pay you, though."

She said, "Don't be silly. I run a general store, not a beanery. Why don't you see to your mount out front while I lock up? My place is the white frame cottage."

He went out to lead Strawberry to the smithy. "I'd like my mare fed and watered," he told the blacksmith. Then he walked along the wagon trace and followed the flagstones to the green-painted door of Polly Clark's modest white cottage.

The door opened before he could knock. Polly Clark waved him into her front parlor and sat him on a leather davenport in front of her cold fireplace, saying, "I'll only be a minute warming up the coffee. I hope you don't mind potato salad and cold meat? It's such a hot, sticky day, after all that rain we've been having."

As soon as he was alone he hauled off his moist boots and wet socks. His feet were fishbelly white and prune-wrinkled. The dry wool socks he had just bought felt a lot better, even inside sort of soggy boots.

The redheaded widow woman rejoined him, carrying a big tray to put down on the bitty table near the sofa. He had naturally hung his hat up by now, but just as naturally kept his frock coat on. She said, "You must feel stuffy in that heavy tweed, Custis. Go on and take it off."

He peeled down to his shirtsleeves and they dug in. Since both were country-raised, they didn't try to chat as they did so. The sliced meat was starting to turn, but her potato salad, at least, was fresh, and her coffee was strong, though a mite acid from standing on the stove since morning. He knew few saloons offered better fare. Once they had cleaned their plates she carried them out and came back with a peach cobbler that made up for her earlier shortcomings. It even made the coffee taste better. She made him have two slices and told him it was all right to smoke afterwards.

He lit up. She carried the tray back to the kitchen and rejoined him on the sofa, saying, "Nobody will want anything from my store at high noon. How long can you visit with me, Custis?"

"I'm in no hurry to get sunstroked," he said. "I was just sort of wondering what I should do next. If I head back to Denver without anything better to report, my boss will raise ned with me. On the other hand, them rascals as robbed your post office must be miles from here by now or, even worse, hiding out slick, closer. I can't ask too many questions right now. Not even the leaves are moving out front."

She said, "I know. This town is dead even during working hours. What kind of questions do you still have to ask, Custis?"

"I ain't sure. There's a few loose threads I'd like to pick at, if I knew who to ask about 'em. I might ride back over to the Middle Fork and talk some more to Lefty Page when it cools off. Lefty was the only one who admitted to getting a good look at those robbers. You was getting more stomped on than looking at anyone, and the blacksmith didn't even turn in time."

She sniffed sort of primly and said, "That Hiram Boggs is going to find himself in a whole lot of trouble, any minute, whether he watches out or not."

Longarm said, "Oh? You heard about his friendship with Miss June, too?"

She said, "Just about everyone but that girl's daddy has, by now. Deputy Compten warned him, just last week, that there would be trouble if he didn't start showing a little common sense!"

Longarm frowned thoughtfully. "Compten was the town law who wound up dead in the road right in front of that smithy. But, nope, that don't work. Lefty Page surely would have mentioned it if Compten got gunned by the dirty old man. Have you ever sold anything to an old mountain man called Pappy Garson? Gray-haired but sort of spry? Said he worked at odd jobs here and about?"

She grimaced. "Oh, him. Used to live over near Ward with two young squaws, his daughters. I had to take a broom to him one day when he made an improper remark and then tried to steal from me. Where on earth did you meet *him*, Custis? I heard he'd been run out of Ward years ago."

Longarm nodded soberly. "He'd have been living on Trapper's Rock with his squaw wife before Ward got built. How could you have run him out of your store if he got run out of Ward so long ago?"

She said, "This isn't Ward. He's said to be living in the woods now. He comes through here from time to time. He always says he's looking for work. He's never worked around here, though. Like I said, he's just trash.

Living from hand to mouth as a beggarman or thief."

"You'd have noticed if he was riding or walking the last time you saw him, I hope?"

"As a matter of fact, he came through with a matched pair of handsome black thoroughbreds. Riding one bareback and leading the other. It was . . . let me see . . . a month or so ago, the last time he came through. He came in saying he wanted some ribbon bows. Red and blue, I think. Then he got fresh with me and tried to walk out with a box of shells. That's when I fear I lost my temper."

He said, "I don't blame you. .30-30 shells, Miss Polly?"

She looked surprised. "As a matter of fact, they were." Then she unbuttoned the back of her bodice to let it hang more open under the swept-up hair above the nape of her neck, adding, "My, it sure is getting hot. I hope I won't shock you if I expose a little more of my flesh to the air?"

"Expose all you've a mind to, ma'am. I told you I was a down-home gent. Getting back to ammunition, do you by chance sell .36 pistol rounds?"

She pursed her lips. "I'd have to look. I know nobody has asked for any recently, if that's what you mean."

"That was what I meant. If you ain't sold any, it don't matter whether you have any in stock. I found a fresh .36 round out in the woods not long ago. Might not mean anything. I wasn't *too* close to the trail them robbers took."

She brightened and said, "Oh, I heard all about that

128

when the boys rode in early this morning. They said they'd been following a false lead, and they seemed mighty upset about it."

He noticed she had unbuttoned another button. Her face did look sort of flushed. "They wasn't riding as dumb as they wound up looking. At least one unshod pony, as described by a witness, did turn up on Dead Cow Creek Trail. The mistake the posse made was following the trail where it left the creek. I found the pony upstream a ways, dead."

She said, "Oh, the poor thing. Who do you suppose might have shot it?"

He shrugged. "If I knew that, I wouldn't be sitting here watching a pretty gal undress."

She gasped, "That's a terrible thing to say! You've yet to see anything improper, and I can't help it if the noonday sun seems to be glaring right through the roof at me, can I?"

"Neither can I, and I'm suffering, too," he chuckled. "But so far, all you've said I could take off was my coat."

She giggled coyly. "Well, you can take off your vest and open your shirt, if you promise to be good."

He did so, wondering why gals always told a man to be good while they were smiling wickedly at him. "Speaking of public morals here in Jimtown, who's left to warn that blacksmith about Miss June if Compten's dead and Whitey Jung's been fired?"

"Oh, hadn't you heard? That was all a misunderstanding. Under-Sheriff Love never *fired* Whitey. For one thing, he didn't have the authority. Poor Whitey just got excited when the older lawman twitted him about the way he'd been running his own posse. Whitey's never been noted for his calm temper. But they got it all straightened out once everyone calmed down, and Whitey's still the law here, at least when he has the time. When he's not wearing his badge, he's the foreman of the Lazy W." She added coyly, "So far, I don't think he's too worried about that horrid old blacksmith and that horrid young trashy June. I guess he guesses what people do in private is their own business. How do *you* feel about such matters, Custis?"

"Being federal, I can say right out I find some local blue laws needlessly stuffy," he told her.

Then he took her in his arms and kissed her. She kissed back with enthusiasm and a tongue still sweet from peach cobbler. But as they came up for air she gasped, "Oh, Custis, whatever gave you the notion I wanted you to do that?"

"You did. But it ain't too late to stop if I read your smoke signals wrong," he told her.

This time she kissed him, but she had to record a proper protest. "It's the middle of the day and I have to think about getting back to my store!"

He held her close as he said, "Won't nobody miss you for hours but, all right, how much time have we got?"

"Not enough, I fear."

Then, as he cupped a breast in his palm she sighed and added, "Not here on the sofa, you big goof! What do you think I keep a bed in the next room for?"

He picked her up and carried her in to find out.

130

Chapter 10

The wagon trace back up to Ward got there via a series of tedious zigzags laid out with wagon brakes in mind more than anyone in a hurry. So, having the local scenery down better now, Longarm cut cross-country over hill and dale. Old Strawberry acted as if she found some of the slopes unfriendly, but Longarm explained they were going uphill most of the way, in any case, and only had to whip her with his hat now and again.

Away from second-growth aspen, the slopes were more studded with dwarf evergreen, taller pine, and slower-growing hardwoods, along with more granite boulders of all sizes than open range really needed. Whoever had changed the Shining Mountains to the Rocky Mountains had no doubt seen these parts of it first. He rode between two big boulders on a rise to see the glen beyond was full of grass and cows. The mountain park had likely been cleared of timber and the cows had never found it on their own. He muttered, "Nice little spread," as he rode on down the slope. A calico longhorn with a mean look in its eye moved as if to head them off. "Cut that out, cow," Longarm said. "You're neither a bull nor a watchdog and we don't have time to play tag with you."

The steer sensed he meant it and went back to inhaling the lush green blue-stem it was knee-deep in. Longarm knew the grass had come west along with the cows and nodded his approval. He had seen enough once-rich range abused by poor or thoughtless stockmen in his time. The forty-odd head they were grazing hereabouts was just right for the pretty little glen. Any more, and the grass would have had a time keeping ahead of the beef. Any fewer and aspen would start crowding in.

He saw woodsmoke rising off to his left. It was a mite out of his way, but he was paid to be nosy, so he drifted over that way. Sure enough, he saw a thrifty home spread made of logs and split cedar smiling at him through the trees.

As he rode in he spied two old folks sitting on the porch of the main cabin. The old gent rose to greet him as the old woman in the faded purple mother hubbard just kept rocking. He liked them on first sight, for there was not a trace of meanness nor suspicion in either sweet old dried-apple face as he reined in and introduced himself.

They turned out to be Mom and Pop Campbell. At least, that was what they said everybody called them. He said he was sorry to say he couldn't stay and coffee and cake some with them, as he was in a hurry. "I couldn't help noticing them cows up the slope was branded Lazy W. I understand your ramrod's Whitey Jung?"

132

The old lady beamed and said Whitey was a darling boy. The old man was canny enough to ask what Longarm wanted with Whitey.

Longarm said, "Nothing unfriendly, sir. As you doubtless know, Whitey and me was up on Long's Peak last night. He left before I got a chance to compare notes with him on that post office robbery."

Pop Campbell nodded. "We know all too well about that holdup, son. We had the modest profits of our last beef sales in Miss Polly's safe."

His wife said, "I've been meaning to visit Jimtown and see if that poor girl is all right. The boys say she got knocked down and halfways out by those wicked robbers."

"She's feeling fine, ma'am," Longarm told her. "I know because I just left her, looking mighty fit. I don't see Whitey about at the moment."

Pop Campbell said, "He's out looking for them outlaws and our money. I let him take Slim Tracey and Spud McArtle with him. He said something about scouting Trapper's Rock."

"Do tell? Now that you mention it, I have heard Trapper's Rock is a suspicious place. How would one get there from here?"

The old man pointed. "Keep going till you get near the Evans spread. Don't go all the way. There's a fair-sized lake up yonder. Trapper's Rock is just this side of her. It's so called because in the old days it made a good place for the beaver boys to fort up. Not too far from water and a good field of fire from the top. Whitey said he'd heard tales of an old thief who used to live on

Trapper's Rock. It was a long time ago. But he thought it might be worth a look, in case anyone else recalls what a fine hideout Trapper's Rock would make. It's a mile or more off any well-traveled trail, you see. Nobody near there but the Evans hands, and they got a whole lake between them and the rock, so—"

Longarm cut in to say he thought Whitey's notion made a heap of sense. Then he asked, in a more cautious tone, "I was given to understand Slim Tracey and McArtle don't like to ride with old Whitey much. That might have been why they dropped out of his posse the other night."

Pop Campbell chuckled indulgently and said, "Oh, Slim gets mad and quits at least three times a week. Spud just goes along with him. They don't really mean it. You see, both Whitey and Slim are sort of proud and proddy. Whitey's a top hand. I'd never have made him ramrod if he didn't know what he was doing. But he do have a temper and he can be short with anyone who makes a mistake. Slim and Spud are good cowhands, too, but not as good as Whitey. So he has to rawhide 'em some. Spud knows his place, but Slim's young and ain't found it yet. So when someone tells him he's a total idjet he tends to get upset. He knows better than to talk back to Whitey. Whitey tends to hit first and argue later. So old Slim just storms off to sulk a spell until Spud can talk him into coming back."

"Well, it's your crew, Pop," Longarm said. "Since they all seem to be fond of one another again, would you know what that fuss they had the other night was about?"

134

"Sure. Whitey thought Slim had been acting too brave. He'd already warned Slim and Spud not to ride on ahead so much. Then, when they rushed a cabin without orders, Whitey commenced to cloud up and rain on 'em good in front of the others. Slim got sore, as usual, and the rest you know. He's promised not to do that no more. If they're still speaking to one another they'll have made it to Trapper's Rock by now. You'll meet 'em coming back, if you hurry."

Longarm said he would and rode on. Not wanting to get lost off the mental map he was packing in his head, he decided to cut directly to the next bend of the wagon trace and ask directions to the Evans spread for openers.

They got there, but there seemed to be nobody on the road when they reached it. It was cool enough among the trees, but the wider gravel road was baking, with the sun glaring almost straight down through the thin mountain air. Longarm could see enough smoke for a small town rising to his right. That had to be Ward. The Evans spread was likely the other way.

But he didn't get there that afternoon. He barely made it across the road to cover as a swarm of rapid-fire bees commenced to buzz around him and Strawberry.

The frisky mare didn't have to be heeled to light out fast, but he heeled her anyway. He flattened out atop her just as some son of a bitch got the range and sent one through the space where his back would have been had he not ducked in time.

They they were crashing through aspen, making more noise than the distant gunshots had, so he reined in, tied up, and went back afoot with his Winchester to

135

see if anyone still loved him.

There was nothing on or across the wagon trace but dead silence until a grasshopper buzzed and made Long-arm freeze even more. He stayed that way a long time, peering out from the cover of the roadside brush. Then he called out, "I see you. Come out with your hands full of sky and we'll talk about it, hear?"

No answer. He shrugged. It seldom worked, but it was always worth a try. He eased back, rose, and headed back to where he'd left his mount. He stopped when he saw fresh sap oozing from the pale bark of a fair-sized aspen and put his Winchester aside to get out his pocketknife. Aspen wood dug easily. It was half air and water and didn't burn worth much. It only took him a few minutes and a lot of cursing to dig out the slug. It was a .36 pistol round.

He pocketed the evidence and went on to find Straw-berry. When he did he told her, "I thought that was about ten shots. That was why he missed us despite all the lead he was throwing. Them long-barrel Navy Colts are accurate enough, but they still throw pistol lead. What was after us was a two-gun man who don't know the War's been over fifteen years. Old-timer, set in his ways, or a younger sprout who likes to look like Buffalo Bill when he ain't gunning yellow-streaked."

He mounted up and headed for Ward through the woods. He had given them a fair crack at his back in tall timber. It would be interesting to see how close a two-gun man wearing antiques could get to him in the open.

* * *

Ward was a little larger and more substantial than Jimtown. On riding in, the first impression Longarm had was that there was a bank holdup in progress. But as he tethered Strawberry on the safe side of a water trough he decided bank robbers hardly ever screamed so shrill. So he left his sixgun holstered as he eased along the plank walk to see what all the fuss might be about.

What it was about, he discovered upon entering the bank, was a dispute about the passbook Star and Feather Garson were waving at the stone face of a smug-looking banker who'd come around the tellers' cages.

Feather spotted Longarm first. She sobbed, "Oh, praise the Lord! We're saved!"

Star turned, too, to yell, "Make this son of a bitch give us our money, Custis!"

Longarm asked the banker why they were carrying on like that. The stout, stone-faced dude said, "It's very simple, whoever you are. They don't have any money in this bank."

Longarm took the passbook from Star, looked it over, and decided, "Sure they do. It says so, here, in plain English, that one Cedric Garson—dumb as the name may sound—has eight hundred and seventy-nine dollars and thirty-six cents on deposit in this here bank. He's listed his daughters, Star and Feather, as his co-depositers. That was smart of him. I know for a fact that these young ladies is Star and Feather Garson. And before you call me a liar I'd best show you my own badge and I.D."

The banker seemed unimpressed by his credentials as well. He told Longarm, "That may well be. I'd heard Garson was a squaw man. But he had no right to deposit money in the name of . . . well, what *else* would you call these two?"

"Next of kin, who unlike you, *knew* who their father might have been," Longarm growled.

"Are you calling me a bastard, Deputy?" the banker sputtered.

"If you don't want the name, don't play the game. You never objected to Pappy Garson's kin when you took his money, did you? Each one of them deposits is stamped as properly deposited in this fool bank. Each time you or one of your tellers took the money and entered it in his passbook, the names of his daughters was right there, plain to see. So what's this all about?"

"Nobody ever told us they were *Indians!*" the banker said.

Longarm snorted in disgust. "How many Irish gals named Star and Feather bank here, you silly cuss? Besides, they can't be more'n *half* Kimoho. So it ain't gonna work."

The banker blustered, "The law is very firm on that point. No white man not licensed by the Bureau of Indian Affairs is allowed to do business involving more than twenty dollars with a ward of the federal government. This institution is not licensed by the B.I.A. to deal with Indians. We are chartered by the State of Colorado under both state and federal banking regulations to—"

"Aw, stop flapping your fat lips," Longarm cut in.

"We all know what you're trying to pull and, like I said, it ain't gonna work. These gals ain't wards of nobody. Their mother's nation is officially extinct and they was raised white, sort of. That makes 'em free, half-white, and over twenty-one, in Miss Star's case, at least. An unmarried woman is allowed to handle her own money. So give 'em the damned money. I know they'll likely spend it foolish, but it's still theirs, and, as an officer of the law, it's my duty to see they ain't robbed. So just don't rob them an we'll all stay friends."

"This may be a matter for the courts to decide," the banker tried. "How do I know either of them is a legal adult? They just told me their father is dead. The probate court will want to see his death certificate, their birth certificates, and, of course, a valid marriage license proving them his lawful heirs—"

"There you go again," Longarm cut in as, somewhere back in the cages, someone else stifled a laugh.

As the banker stopped, red-faced but still determined-looking, Longarm said, "Let's try this another way. We're talking less than a thousand dollars here. A fortune for these little gals, but chicken-feed to even a country bank, I hope. The sign out front says you're capitalized to a quarter million. I sure hope you are, for should the bank examiners find you've been bragging, someone could be in a whole lot of trouble. It's against the law for a bank to assure its depositors they got more money on hand than they really have. I know most do. It pays to advertise snake oil, too. But in this case, you'd sure better be able to back that gilt-letter brag, friend."

The banker looked more ashen than red now. "Don't try to threaten us, you fool. You're only a deputy marshal, not a bank examiner!"

Longarm nodded pleasantly. "That's true. I'm a federal agent up here to investigate a robbery. The robbers is still at large. Need I say more?"

"I don't know what you're trying to do. We heard about that post office robbery over in Jimtown. What has that to do with us?"

Longarm sighed. "Right. I need to say more. A lot of money just got stolen. It's my considered opinion that somebody with that much money might feel safer with it in some bank. You got the only bank for miles. I don't know much about such matters, but who knows what we might find out if I asked the bank examiners for their professional help in such complicated financial transactions? I stand ready to swear under oath, in state or federal court, that you folk struck me as mighty casual about proper deposits and withdrawals. Lord only knows who might have deposited a larger sum with you, recent. You don't seem to honor your own passbooks."

The banker looked sick. "Did I hear you say that was your *considered* opinion, as of this discussion?" he asked.

Longarm said, "You did. Give them their damned money and we'll say no more about it."

The banker gulped. "We can't. Not all of it. Eight hundred would empty the safe." His hitherto cold eyes were pleading as he asked Star, "Could you take, say, two hundred now, and come back for the rest after roundup time?"

Star looked to Longarm for guidance. "Take it," he said. "If you blow a whole two hundred in lessn'n two months you're better off with most of it still in the bank."

"But, Custis, you just showed us he was trying to crook us!"

Longarm smiled wolfishly at the small-town big shot as he told her, "He won't do that again. He's likely telling the truth about being strapped this time of the year, when everyone's borrowing and nobody's putting nothing in. Make a modest withdrawal today. Make it a matter of passbook record that this bank considers you a valid depositor. If they try it again, come fall, get a lawyer and, if you can't get a lawyer, go the nearest Indian agent and allow you're a poor picked-on Indian. Either way, you'll cause more than six hundred dollars' worth of trouble for this bank, and I'd say this gent is a reasonable cuss. Ain't that right, cuss?"

The banker proved he was reasonable indeed and even told the girls he was sorry about the slight misunderstanding. As they left with Longarm, Star said, "That was swell of you, Custis. You want to go off in the woods with me for some fun now?"

He said, "Not hardly. I want you to keep that money inside your calico, and your calico on, till you can get it to a safe place. You still staying up on the mountain?"

Feather said, "No. We come down after planting Pappy so we could live more civilized. That's why we needed the money. How come you never want to screw us? Don't you like us?"

Her sister told her, "Don't be an idjet! Didn't you

141

just watch him holding up a bank for us? Of course he likes us. He's a good old boy."

Longarm assured them of his undying devotion and then, hoping he'd seen the last of them, left Strawberry tethered where she was as he scouted up the local law.

Deputy Westlake was an older and wiser-looking version of the law over in Jimtown, even if Longarm did find him in the saloon after asking all about for him. Westlake bought Longarm a beer and, while willing enough to go over recent events, he was unable to shed much light on them. He said, "Me and my boys set up a picket line, like Jimtown asked. But they never come our way and we never seen fit to join the posses up to Long's Peak. Anyone could see that was a red herring."

"How so, pard?"

"Shoot, they had to know this country to know that post office was worth robbing. We got a bank right down the street if we're discussing crooked wayfaring strangers."

"I just had a word with 'em. They don't have much money on hand this time of the year."

Westlake inhaled some suds. "There you go. Only a local would know that. Says right out front they're local. And who but a local would know all that money was stored so casual in a crossroads post office? Does Miss Polly have a sign out front saying she keeps lots of cash in the back?"

"Matter of fact, the sign says she's having a going-out-of-business sale," Longarm said.

Westlake nodded. "I heard. It's tough. She's a good old gal, but she wouldn't have lost her job as postmistress if she hadn't got robbed, and she wouldn't have got robbed had not someone known she had more than petty cash on hand."

Longarm said, "Lefty Page said he saw an unshod paint under one of the robbers, and an unshod paint did go up the Dead Cow Creek Trail. I know that because I found it up there, shot in the head."

Westlake shrugged and said, "They sent a rider to tell us they was on the robber's trail. We knew better. Now you do, too. Can't you see what they pulled? They split up just outside of Jimtown. One or more led the tell-tale paint up a trail to nowheres, got rid of it, and just went on home or, hell, joined the fool posse. Whitey Jung's a good kid. But who needs kids? He made a damn fool of himself, wiring the whole world he had mounted outlaws trapped on Long's Peak, for God's sake!"

Longarm grimaced. "Well, he made *us* look dumb, too. By the way, what's the story on Trapper's Rock? Last I heard of Whitey he was scouting there for the post office robbers."

Westlake laughed. "Only robbers around Trapper's Rock, these days, would be pack rats. It's too close to the Evans spread to use as a hideout and, before you ask, yes, the Evans boys are part-time deputies of mine and, no, they couldn't have been in on the robbery. They were here in Ward at the time, loading a buckboard, in plain view of God and me and everybody."

Longarm shrugged and said, "I'll take your word on them, then. What sort of a reputation does Lefty Page enjoy?"

Westlake laughed again. "I ain't sure he'd *enjoy* it.

143

But he's never been known to steal anything more serious than another man's gal. Lefty's all right. He don't even lie about horseflesh, and in these parts that's considered almost sissy."

Longarm nodded and said, "Men who fib about other matters generally start with horses. So let's assume everything he said about the little he witnessed that noisy few minutes was true. He said the dying deputy said something odd: 'Who would have ever thought it?' Thought what? He must have known he was *shot*."

"It could have come as some surprise to him," Westlake opined. "On the other hand, if he recognized even one of the owlhoots coming at him, he might have considered it a thing to wonder about."

Longarm said, "Yeah. It makes more sense to me that way, too. Lefty said some of the riders in front might have let their face masks slip. It's beginning to look more and more like an inside job to me."

"Hell, I figured that from the beginning," Westlake said. "Miss Polly had the money locked in a safe. They took no more than a few seconds to clean it out before she could even sit up and study them some. That adds up to someone knowing the combination."

"Miss Polly can't recall who that might have been."

"Hell, what does *she* know about stickups? She's just a gal. That safe has been there a long time. Who's to say when or how often someone else has watched her open and close it?"

Longarm frowned thoughtfully and said, "A really experienced crook might have been able to guess better by listening to the clicks. I hear tell Pappy Garson had

144

sticky fingers, and he was in her general store now and again. What do you think?"

Westlake shook his head. "Too big a job for the likes of old Garson. He's been suspected of high-grading up-guarded mine shafts and selling horses casual, with no bill of sale. I can't see him as part of a *killing* gang. For one thing, he was too shy. I'd say they was wild young rascals from around here. We've been keeping an eye out for sudden spending. So far, they've been too smart, but give 'em time. Sooner or later some hand making a dollar a day is bound to show up in a pair of braggy chaps or fancy Mexican spurs, and that's when we'll nail 'em."

Longarm didn't want to wait that long. He thanked Westlake for his words of cheer and got Strawberry to ride on back to the scene of the crime. If nobody connected with the robbery had headed for Ward, Ward could be scratched off, he hoped.

He rode more slowly through the woods now, even though it was downhill. He reined in from time to time to have a serious look behind him, and when he was moving he had his Winchester out and across his thighs with a round in the chamber.

He figured he'd make it about two-thirds of the way when a distant fusillade of gunfire echoed through the trees around him.

That gave him pause. But since the faraway shot could hardly been meant for him, he rode on. He was still on the prod when he rode out on the wagon trace just outside Jimtown and spotted another rider coming his way at a full gallop. It was Lefty Page.

145

Lefty slid his paint to a halt near Strawberry and yelled, "You're just the man I was riding to see! Miss Polly said you'd rid up to Ward and we sure need some serious law and order in Jimtown right now. Whitey Jung and his boys are there, of course, but we've already established what I think of Whitey as a lawman."

As they rode on together Longarm said, "I heard the shots. Was it another robbery or a shootout?"

"Shootout, towards the last," Lefty said. "Old Peckerwood Sam caught his daughter, June, with the blacksmith. The results was as much as we'd all warned that fool blacksmith. Then one of Whitey's deputies nailed Peckerwood Sam as he was running from the scene of slaughter, gun in hand."

Longarm grimaced. "Such domestic disputes are a pain in the ass to any lawman. I'd say the case was Whitey's entirely. All they need is a corroborating statement from the daughter for the county coroner's office. It ain't like either her dead lover or her dead father aim to dispute her word."

Lefty shook his head. "June ain't in no position to give a statement, now. She was hit in the head. Her brains was blowed out."

Longarm nodded grimly. "You say Whitey and his boys were in town to terminate Peckerwood Sam's killing spree? That's odd. I was told they were over by Ward, scouting Trapper's Rock."

"They might have been, earlier," Lefty said. "I was in the saloon when all hell busted loose. By the time me and the others could get there, it was all over. Hearing the same shots and being closer, Whitey took the front

146

entrance and Slim Tracey went around the back. Slim hit the jackpot. Took a bullet through his hat. Then he shot better, and that was the end of it. We carried all three bodies to the root cellar behind the saloon. It was me as told Whitey he had to send word to the county and see what they aimed to do about it. When things get unsettled, old Whitey tends to give a mighty good imitation of a chicken with its head lopped off."

Chapter 11

The improvised Jimtown morgue smelled more of pota-
toes and turnips than of death. The three bodies lined up
on the dirt floor hadn't been dead long enough to smell.

The two dead men looked as dumb, helpless, and
sort of embarrassed as dead men usually look. Some
thoughtful soul had pulled the blacksmith's pants up for
him.

The girl who'd died with them looked somehow
deader and more obscene, even with her thin body
wrapped in a tarp. Her mouth was softly smiling, as if
she was keeping a secret to herself. She probably was.
Her long-lashed eyelids were partway open and Longarm had the discomforting feeling she was peeking as he
dropped to one knee beside her for a closer look. Behind him, Whitey Jung said, "You can see where the
bullet went in and out."

Longarm didn't answer. The young woman's hair
was matted with drying blood down the left side of her
skull. The little blue hole in her right temple was surrounded by a dark halo of powder burn. He gingerly

lifted a corner of the tarp to see that she'd died wearing a cheap shift made of flour sacking, at least.

He muttered, "Old Peckerwood Sam sure must have had a suspicious nature if it was broad day and they was both dressed more or less decent."

The younger deputy shook his head and said, "The wonder was that it took him so long to find out. To tell the truth, a lot of people figured the old drunk just didn't care. June's mother died a couple of years ago and the girl was sort of left to shift for herself by her shiftless old dad. But I reckon any dad would be upset by the sight of his daughter with some dirty old man. I know *I* would."

Longarm saw the smith had been hit just over the right eye. Longarm tried to picture the way it had happened. He shrugged and said, "It works if we credit an outraged father with good marksmanship as well as a certain amount of sudden strictness."

"Old Sam was good with a gun when he was sober," Whitey said. "That wasn't often. But he must have been sober when he decided to do something at last about his wicked daughter."

Longarm nodded, but said, "Drunk or sober, the usual instinct in such a situation is to kill the man and beat the shit out of the female. But let that go. It's established that Peckerwood Sam was an unusual father."

Longarm stared down at the lean, unshaven face of Peckerwood Sam. It might have been a nice-looking face once. Years of hard living and a bullet hole smack between the eyes hadn't improved Sam's looks worth mention. "Your sidekick's a fine shot, too," Longarm said.

Whitey said, "He had to be. Sam fired first and drilled a hole in old Slim's hat. Slim saw no reason to argue the matter further. Yeah, Slim's always been good with a gun."

Longarm rose, dusting off his pant leg. "I noticed. You wouldn't know what kind of gun Slim packs, would you? I see you favor an army issue Colt .45."

Whitey said, "I think Slim packs an S&W and a Harrington Richardson. Both .38s. I never paid much attention till I was writing it all down just now. You can ask him. He's sort of steadying his nerves in the saloon, upstairs, with old Spud."

Longarm said, "I will. Let's go. By the way, how is Spud McArtle heeled this afternoon?"

Whitey said, "That's easy. Old Spud is always showing off his old Colt '74. He won it in a card game years ago. It's silver-mounted with ivory grips. Ain't that a bitch?"

As they were going up the steps Whitey went on to ruin a grand notion and give Longarm something else to ponder when he added lightly, "The murder weapons was sort of pretty, too. Parkerised black with all sorts of engravings on 'em. Even sailing ships on the wheels."

"Oh, shit, are we talking a Navy Colt .36?"

"I know they's Colts. I never been in no navy. I figured the bore for .38 or so. Ain't .36 a mite unusual?"

Longarm sighed. "It is now. Used to be more popular. I don't suppose you'd know whether anyone else in these parts packs one or more .36 conversions?"

"Hell, I didn't know Peckerwood Sam did, until just now."

Longarm didn't answer. They climbed out, walked the short way to the saloon, and entered via the back door next to the built-in outhouse.

Inside, Slim and Spud were bellied to the bar along with some of Kincaid's dragoons and other well-wishers, mostly out-of-work miners and part-time cowhands. As Longarm and Whitey joined them, Longarm asked if he could see the gun Slim had used on Peckerwood Sam. The slender young cowhand drew it, show-boat, and twirled it on its trigger guard for inspection. Longarm saw it was indeed an S&W .38. He didn't ask to see the other gun. Anyone could see the nickel-plated revolver was an H&R, and they had never made a .36 to date. It would have been impolite to comment on Slim's mismatched guns and cheap gun rig with misfit holsters. On what Slim likely made off Mom and Pop Campbell he was lucky his boots matched. Both his guns were .38s, and that was what Longarm was most interested in.

Whitey said the .36s they had found in the weeds near Peckerwood Sam had been put away in his saddle-bags for safekeeping. He offered to go get them. Long-arm shook his head and said, "I know what a navy conversion looks like. I've reason to believe Sam was packing two when we seem to have met up earlier today."

He signaled the barkeep for a round of drinks as he went on, "He surely must have had a lot on his mind. I

152

can see a man out to bushwhack the law. I can see a man out to avenge his family honor. Feeling both ways at the same time would call for a sort of unusual disposition."

Spud McArtle said, "Oh, he was a moodsome cuss, all right. It depended on what he'd been drinking, I reckon. The reason he could never hold a job, aside from being a drunk, I mean, was his unpredictable temper. One day he'd be smiling and friendly as hell, and the next time you seen him he'd call you a son of a bitch."

The barkeep had picked up on the conversation as he poured. "That's the plain unvarnished truth, Deputy Long," he chimed in. "We refused him service here after he kept starting fights or tried to pimp for his girl, depending on whether he'd been drinking or wanted to."

Longarm frowned. "You mean he might have known, ahead, about his daughter and the dumb blacksmith?" he asked.

The barkeep said, "He must have. I did, and I seldom had cause to go anywhere near the smithy."

Spud said, "He did look sort of glaze-eyed, coming out with gun in hand and that silly grin on his fool face."

"You saw the shootout?" Longarm asked.

"Sure. The last part, leastways. Me and Whitey, here, was just watering our ponies near the smithy when the first shots rung out. Whitey said something like 'oh, shit' and we run that way. I seen Whitey was heading in the front way. I made for the side door. Slim, here, beat us all around to the back. Old Slim can move when he

153

has to. Next thing I knowed, Slim's hat was off on its own and he was slapping leather. So I run past the side door and there was Peckerwood Sam just out the back door and then Slim nailed him before I could. Ain't it funny how everything slows down when it's the last time anyone would want to be moving slow? I don't know how old Slim gets around that, but he does. My own gun hand was moving through maple syrup no matter how hard I pushed it, while Slim was a blur of pure speed. Don't never slap leather with old Slim. He's *good*."

Longarm handed Slim's .38 back without comment, but said, "I'm sort of interested in time, this afternoon. I'm trying to place everyone else as I was moving about more sedate. If Peckerwood Sam pegged shots at me earlier near Ward, he must have beat you three back from Trapper's Rock by minutes and— Yeah, it works out. I spent some time in Ward, after. Sam had time to mosey back, mayhaps still mad about missing me, and worked his fool self into a killing rage by the time you three drifted in just ahead of me. The question, now, is why he'd want to gun *me*, of all people. I didn't know him and I for certain never messed with his daughter."

Whitey suggested, "He might have been within a short ride of Trapper's Rock for more serious reasons, spotted you, and come to the conclusion you was near there to scout it as well."

Longarm sipped some beer and said, "That makes sense. You boys might have been lucky it was my back he spotted and not your own. What did you find up there, by the way?"

"Nothing proving anything," Whitey said. "Someone had camped there recent. We found a dead fire up in the hollow atop the rocks. Trapper's Rock is really a big pile of boulders, not just one rock. We found boot heels where someone went down to the nearby lake for water. Later, we rid over to the Evans spread and asked Pop Evans what he might know about it. He said none of his boys had noticed nothing and they wasn't missing any stock. That leaves saddle tramps just passing through, or mayhaps someone more sinister. The fire had been laid before that stormy spell we just had, but not long before. I know the law up at Ward says nobody could have got through them. But what the hell, they got through *us*, didn't they?"

Longarm nodded. "I thought you boys might have gone to Trapper's Rock because you'd heard about that old mountain man with a rep for being crooked."

Whitey nodded back. "Him, too. Who told you about that old hoss thief, Pappy Garson?"

"Lots of folk. He seems to have been a local legend."

"I've been saying all along he was in on that robbery," Slim said. "They say he's been haunting Long's Peak since he got run off Trapper's Rock for screwing Indians and stealing horses."

Whitey looked pained and said, "I wish you'd let us forget Long's Peak, Slim. I saw them unshod pony prints, too. But anyone can see, now, they only went a little ways up Dead Cow Creek Trail. Nobody's been on Trapper's Rock, neither, since that rainy spell. So while they may not be forgotten, they are sure as hell *gone!*"

Longarm saw the conversation was starting to circle.

He politely refused the drink Whitey wanted to buy him, said he'd be back later, and headed for the front door. He noticed Lefty Page drinking alone near the batwings and asked how come. Lefty shrugged and said, "Let them showboat down to the other end all they like. I heard Spud bragging on how ferocious Slim is, just now. He's full of shit. I backed Slim down at a dance one time. It was easy."

"Oh? You're even faster on the draw, Lefty?"

"Don't know. They made us check our guns at the door. So it was a fist city discussion. Slim didn't want to go and I got to take the gal home. She turned out to be tougher than he was."

Longarm smiled in a fatherly way and said, "I wouldn't do that again, Lefty. Slim's killed his man now, and seems to be enjoying his new rep. Lots of men who ain't up to fistfighting can be dangerous as hell with a gun in their hand. Kid Antrim's been proving that down New Mexico way of late. Skinny little bastard couldn't lick a woman in a fistfight. But you know what they say about Sam Colt creating all men equal."

"I ain't afraid of Slim," Lefty groused.

Longarm passed him by and stepped out on the walk. It wouldn't have been polite to tell Lefty *he* was talking like a fool, too.

Longarm went next to the general store. He found Polly Clark alone inside despite her big sale sign. She offered to close up early. He thanked her for her kind offer, but said, "I fear I may be needed back at that root cellar before long. Matt Kincaid ought to be bringing that other body in before sundown, and the county will be sending someone up from Boulder to look into that domestic dispute down at the smithy. You heard about that, of course?"

"Did I ever! The gunshots rattled my front window. I always knew something like that was bound to happen. I told you the girl wasn't nearly as discreet about such matters as I am."

He smiled fondly at her. "Maybe later. I wanted to have another look around in back."

She said, "You can't. The army padlocked the door. Some Post Office men should be here any time now to impound everything. Meanwhile you can't mail or get mail here. I can't even get at the stamps, let alone show you around back there."

"Sure you can," he said, as he rolled over the counter to her side and led the way back. He studied the padlocked door at the far end as he drew his .44-40. Then he said, "Noise might draw a crowd. You got a crowbar handy? Claw-hammer will do."

She reached up on a back shelf for one even as she said, "I don't want to get in trouble, Custis."

"Oh, Matt won't raise too much hell, even if he finds out. We can always replace this lock with another one from your stock."

Before she could argue he had broken the cheap lock open. "There you go. I want to sort of reconstruct the crime. So why don't you go in first and I'll start by jawing through your window cage with you."

She said she was sure they would both wind up in federal prison, but did as he commanded. Once they were in position on either side of the partition he said,

"Good. For openers, I want you to unlock that safe."

She said, "It hasn't been shut since the robbery. They told me to leave everything as it was."

"Even better. I want you to lock it and then unlock it as I listen from here."

She shrugged and moved from the window to do so. By craning his neck he could just make out her shapely rump as she knelt in front of the safe. He couldn't see the safe. He could her the tumblers clicking, barely.

When she'd finished his experiment and stood up, Longarm vaulted the counter to join her inside. He said, "All right. I want you to show me exactly where you was while they come in and out."

She nodded and threw herself down on the floor, half under the counter, her skirt half up to expose more of her than some considered proper. "I was about like this, of course."

He lay down beside her. She said, "Oh, Custis, *here?*"

He laughed. "I'm trying to see what you might have seen from this position. You're sure your feet was aimed at the door like this?"

"Of course. They knocked me down, hard, the moment they barged in. But I wasn't *that* confused. Why?"

"Can't watch the safe door good from this position. Looking up from here in such a narrow space I can see why you couldn't give much of a description."

She said, "I remember blue denim, and one of them was wearing gunmetal spurs. I think I remember flashes of red bandanna. Three or maybe four came back here. If there were others they were out front all the time."

He nodded and said, "Yeah, watching your hired help and their ponies. Then they all rode like hell and Deputy Compten made the mistake of trying to stop half a dozen fast men with one slow gun. We can get up now."

"Do we have to, darling?" she purred.

He laughed. "We'd better. I'd have a hell of a time explaining *that* to Matt Kincaid. He's likely to feel testy enough about the lock if we don't replace it fast."

They got up, replaced the lock with a new one from her stock, and saw they'd timed it just about right when a dragoon came in with his carbine at port to say, "Oh, it's you, Deputy Long. I thought I heard funny noises as I was supping in the tent out back."

Polly smiled at him. "We were just closing up."

The soldier nodded and ducked back out. Longarm said, "You can go home if you want to. The day's about shot. But I hope you won't feel hurt if I head back to the saloon, now."

"Won't you even let me serve you a down-home supper, dear?"

He kissed her but said, "Now, Polly, you know full well what a weak-natured cuss I am."

"I sure hope so. Come on. I promise I won't keep you long."

She lied. It was after sundown when Longarm heard hoofbeats outside the window drapes and pounded her hot flesh faster. She gasped, "Oooooh, nice! But what's the hurry, darling? It's early yet."

He hissed in pleasure. "It's later than you think. I suspect that was Kincaid and his recovery party. The

159

county men and for all we know the Post Office man could already be here. So let's get there so's I can haul my pants on some more, honey."

She moaned, "Don't stop. You're doing fine."

He gasped, fell back down on her heaving breasts, and added, "I sure wish I didn't have to get up now."

She giggled. "How soon can you come back for more, darling?"

He rolled off, swung his feet to the rug, and said, "I don't know. Don't wait up for me. It could be a long night."

"Even longer if you can't get back to me, damn it," she said.

Chapter 12

He knew that was going to be a problem as soon as he got back to the saloon. Jimtown had no town hall, so all important civic affairs were conducted in the one place always open. It could have been worse, Longarm knew. He'd spent many a dull day in a more formal county or federal courthouse.

He found Matt Kincaid seated at a table near the silent piano with two older gents dressed half-city and half-cow. The other army men were drinking at the bar with the townies and three local deputies. Whitey Jung came over to join them as Kincaid introduced the sissier-looking gents as Inspectors Kirby and Stein from the Post Office Department. Kirby was big and soft. Stein was short, lean, and sort of mean-looking. The younger army man told Longarm, "We had one hell of a time recovering Hampshire's body. It was sort of scattered among the rocks where he finally landed. But I don't think we left any important parts on the mountain. They told us about those other bodies in the root cellar out back. I'm sort of sorry I missed the fun."

Longarm said, "It wasn't much fun." Then he turned to the Postal Inspectors to say, "Inspector Polk no doubt told you the details of his pard's death, right?"

Stein said flatly, "Gus Polk doesn't work for the Postmaster General any more. A man's supposed to stand by his pard, not run away. We're obliged to you, Longarm. Gus Polk was still a shit."

The more amiable Kirby said, "We're not really up here to worry about poor old Hamp, sad as we feel about the way he bounced. All the bodies will be buck-boarded down to Boulder in the morning for the medical examiners to mess with. We'll have a new postmaster appointed here in Jimtown in a day or so. The captain, here, assures us nothing's been moved at the scene of the crime."

Kincaid said, "Not if the guards I posted know what's good for them."

Longarm lit a cheroot to give himself time to think. He decided honesty could be the best policy in dealing with halfway reasonable gents. "I had another look in the back of Miss Polly's store this afternoon, Matt. I would have asked your permission had you been here, of course, but you wasn't. So I just did. I replaced the lock afterwards."

Kincaid, knowing Longarm of old, didn't seem too surprised. The Post Office men scowled at him.

Stein snapped, "You had no right to do that! That robbery was strictly a Post Office matter!"

"Yeah. Meanwhile, the only Post Office official was sprawled on the floor, the town law was dead, and his junior deputies was screwing up whether they meant well or not," Longarm replied.

Kirby looked pained and said, "Look, we've thanked both War and Justice for such help as they gave, whether we asked for it or not."

"As well you should have," Longarm said. "The two men you sent up from Boulder showed up late, got killed, or ran away. I figure Matt, here, has done about all soldiers could be at all expected to. But I'm still on the case."

Stein snapped, "The hell you are! Federal marshals may or may not be called in on such matters if we don't have the manpower to handle a case of interference with the U.S. Mail. But in this case we do, and—"

"You're full of shit," Longarm cut in.

As it got sort of tense, Kincaid said softly, "I'm still with you, pard."

Longarm shook his head. "No, thanks. There's no reason for the army to mess about up here when for all we know the Apache could rise any minute. I agree Whitey, here, might have acted sort of excited when he found himself chasing bandits with the help of part-time law. But he did. So I'm here, and—"

"It's not your case. It's ours," Stein cut in.

Whitey Jung, who'd been listening quietly in as much confusion as courtesy, said, "You gents can forget about me and mine, then, if such matters are to be fought over like a durned old bone! I formed a posse and went after the rascals because I thought somebody should, not to steal stealers from anybody."

Longarm nodded at Whitey and said, "You done right, despite your lack of experience with jurisdiction.

163

Your superior had just been gunned. You were the only law left within miles. You'd have been a *real* fool had you just stood there with a finger in your mouth, Whitey. So shut up and listen and you might learn something. Lord knows you don't know much."

Longarm turned back to Stein. "The stamps and envelopes you've impounded are all yours. The money that was stolen is another matter. It wasn't federal funds. It was owned by folks in and about this little town."

"That's why we've discharged Mrs. Clark," Kirby said. "She had no right to serve as a banker as well as postmistress."

"That's what I just said. I'll allow the money in that safe was Post Office business, right or wrong, as long as it had been left for safekeeping in a post office. Once it was out of that safe it was a plain old robbery. The gunning of Deputy Compten was outside Post Office jurisdiction because it took place on a public right-of-way. It belonged to the county of Boulder. Not you. Not me, until the county, in the person of this lawfully appointed deputy sheriff, called on my office for help. My office sent me up here to do something about it. I still aim to. So you two can work with me or against me, but I'm staying on the case until I get the son of a bitch who gunned a fellow peace officer, and you can put that in your pipe and smoke it, or shove it where the sun don't shine. What's it gonna be?"

Stein half rose. Kirby shoved him back in his seat and said, "Look, our job is to arrest those post office robbers and recover their loot, if possible. What if we gave you and Boulder County the one who actually shot that deputy and sort of kept everything else?"

"Depends on who arrests whom," Longarm said. "I'll give you the money when it's recovered. It's finders keepers in the case of any arrests outside or off post office property. Take it or leave it."

"That's not much of a choice, Longarm."

"Sure it is. I said you could have the money if you didn't give me a hard time. If you want to act like idiots I can turn any money I recover over to Whitey, here, and let you all fight it out in court."

The younger deputy said, "Hot damn. Some of that money *is* the property of the nice old folk I *work* for, now that I study on it. What if we was to just give *everyone* back their money, Longarm?"

Kirby looked like he was trying not to vomit as he said, "That is not the way it's done. It has to be done the official way, nitpicky or not." He stared soberly at Longarm for a long, unwinking moment before he said, "Deal. You turn any money you recover over to us and we share the credit for any arrests with you."

It was nice to know which one of them was in charge. Little Stein looked like a hard-cased cuss to get along with even when one agreed with him.

"I don't want to share no paperwork on anyone but the one who gunned a fellow lawman," Longarm said. "I dislike killers personally and that bastard is all mine. Agreed?"

Kirby nodded. It took Stein a little longer. But when he did Longarm turned to Whitey Jung. "I hope you're paying attention, old son. There's more to being a law-

165

man than just tear-assing about with a tin star and a gun. Do you savvy what jurisdiction means now?"

Whitey looked sheepish. "Under-Sheriff Love told me I was young and foolish up on Long's Peak. I'm sorry I raised such a fuss, now."

Longarm told him, not unkindly, "You are sort of young and foolish. All us smart old bastards have to go through that first. I hope you understand that these other gents and me own the rights to them post office robbers and that you and yours can drop out of the game?"

Whitey said, "I never wanted jurisdiction in the first place. I like simpler cases, like the shooting this afternoon here in town. I get to keep that one, right?"

"The coroner's jury will put you down as the first peace officer on the scene. You'll be sorry, once you've had to write it all down more than once. But let's talk about that, too."

"Oh, for God's sake. That dirty story can't be federal!" Stein muttered.

Longarm nodded. "It ain't. It was murder, pure and simple, and Whitey, here, was such town law as there was."

"Gee, thanks," the kid said.

Longarm told Whitey, "The reason I'm bringing this up is twofold. The late Peckerwood Sam was a hand-to-mouth rascal who was willing to sell his own daughter for money. A man like that could do most anything for money, including armed robbery, or at least watching the ponies for his pals, right?"

Whitey nodded. "Sure. I follow your drift, and he did pack a .36!"

Longarm said, "I found a .36 round not too far off the wrong trail your posse followed and I dug a .36 slug out of a tree after it passed me too close for comfort. So, yeah, I am discussing a suspect who gunned Deputy Compten and tried to gun me more than once. You called on me for help, officially, Deputy Jung. So with your permission I'm ready to make an arrest, and how 'bout it?"

Jung blinked in surprise. "Well, hell, sure, but how do you figure to arrest Peckerwood Sam, now? He's dead, ain't he?"

Longarm got to his feet. As Whitey began to rise Longarm pushed him back down and told Matt Kincaid, "Keep him here and watch his hands, will you, Captain?"

Kincaid nodded and smiled pleasantly at the confused Whitey Jung. "In case you're wondering, I got a gun under this table trained in the general direction of your balls. So put both hands on the top of the table and we shall see what we shall see."

Whitey gulped. "What's going on here?"

"I've no idea," Kincaid said, "but Longarm and me have worked together before. It never takes him long once he gets that hunting look in his eye."

It didn't. Longarm strode halfway to the bar, braced his boot heels wide in the sawdust, and called out, "Slim Tracey, I am arresting you in the name of the law, and anything you do or say may and will be used against you. So say what you like and watch what you do. I suggest you start by grabbing some sky."

Slim did no such thing. As everyone but him and

Spud McArtle scattered to get out of the line of fire, Slim went for his guns, and Spud had been right. The kid moved fast as a striking sidewinder.

But Longarm hadn't died from snakebite yet. He beat Slim to the draw, just, and put three rounds in Slim and a fourth in Spud even *faster* than a sidewinder could strike.

Slim went down like a log chopped through close to the ground. Spud slid down the bar, staring in horror through the blue haze of gunsmoke as Longarm said, "Sorry about that, Spud. You should have sent your hands the other way. I gave you both the choice."

Spud muttered, "Aw, gee," and followed his deadlier sidekick to the sawdust.

Longarm holstered his smoking sixgun and knelt between them to feel both their throats. "I hoped to keep Spud alive," he announced. "That's why I shot him low. This other sneaky son of a bitch deserved a slower death, but that's just the way it goes sometimes."

As others began to breathe easier and edge in, Longarm asked Kincaid, "Matt, could we have this place more to ourselves, now?"

Kincaid locked eyes with one of his ashen-faced dragoons and said, "Corporal Miller, I want this taproom cleared, save for the army and the law."

As his soldier moved to shoo everyone else out Kincaid asked, "Can I let this one up, now?" "Sure," Longarm said. "Whitey's all right. I was just concerned he might try to back his outfit without thinking. The three of them all rode for the Lazy W."

As they all rose from the table to join him over the

two on the floor, Longarm said, "Matt, this one might live if he gets some medical attention."

The officer called out to his nearest dragoon, "You heard the man, Douglas. I want a litter in here on the double. Take him to Sergeant Gross and tell them if he dies or escapes they can commend their souls to Jesus, because their asses will be all mine!"

As the soldiers scurried to obey, Inspector Kirby nudged Longarm. "If either of those men you just murdered had anything to do with that post office robbery, we'd like to hear about it now," he said.

Longarm frowned. "Bite your tongue. I gave 'em both a break they'd never have given me, and one of 'em may live long enough to make a statement, least-ways."

Stein said, "We saw the break you gave them just now. Let's talk about why you executed Tracey, not how."

Longarm flicked ash from his cheroot and said, "Let's sit back down then. It's a long story. Barkeep? Could we have us some beer over here?"

Longarm waited until they were all settled before he explained, "I'm almost certain Slim Tracey was the mastermind. I know he was a born killer. None of the others seemed to be. So, yeah, it was him as gunned Deputy Compten when he saw Compten recognized him. Spud McArtle can fill in the other names for us when he feels better, if he knows what's good for him. Three of the six had to be Slim, Spud, and the late Peckerwood Sam."

Whitey Jung protested, "Hold on, Longarm. I may

be young and inexperienced, but I'd hardly call what Slim and Sam tried to do to each other this very afternoon a sign of pure devotion. And, damn it, Slim and Spud was with me, riding *after* the bandits!"

Longarm said, "I ain't done yet. Slim was tired of you riding him as well as with him. But every time he quit in a snit he saw he couldn't get far without money, and jobs are hard to find up here in such hardscrabble cattle country. So the first move Slim made before the dawn before the robbery was to lead an unshod paint pony up Dead Cow Creek, making sure he left plenty of sign, before he shot it higher up and took the Skull Trail back lest he meet anyone else out riding so early. It had to be before dawn because I found the rare pistol round he lost in the dark where he reloaded."

Whitey shook his head stubbornly. "That won't work. Lefty Page says he saw that paint pony after daybreak, when they was riding out after robbing the post office. I know I saw its hoofmarks. For why else would I have followed such a swampy tick-infested trail to Long's Peak of all places?"

Longarm said, "Lefty didn't see *that* paint. He saw another. Unshod Indian ponies ain't hard to come by, and one unshod paint looks much like any other. They might have gotten the idea by watching Pappy Garson riding about aboard a matched pair of horses he stole from Lord knows where. I don't know whether Pappy Garson was in on it or not. He's dead, his kids are nice, and I just don't care."

He wet his whistle with more beer and continued,

"They didn't care where the rest of you thought that false trail led. Once they were out of town they just split up and circled through the woods. At least Slim and Spud rode in innocent to join you as you raved and ranted about a posse."

Whitey gasped and said, "That works! Now that I study back on it, and they *did* get up earlier than me that morning. They told Pop Campbell they'd seen wolf tracks over to our north range and aimed to do something about the critter. I never paid much mind when Pop told me about it over breakfast."

Longarm said, "You couldn't be everywhere at once, and that sweet old couple wouldn't suspect a chicken thief if they saw him in the henhouse. Once Slim had laid a false trail in advance they all got together and hit the post office. Things went sour when they knocked Miss Polly down only to discover she'd locked the safe and they couldn't get it open."

"*Somebody* got it open, damn it. The money was missing and ain't been found yet!" Kirby cut in.

Longarm said, "Let's eat this apple a bite at a time, gents. Remember, none of them were real outlaws. They was just a bunch of impoverished sneaks driven desperate by common greed. It only works if they got rattled, lit out as fast as they come in, and gunned poor Compten as they was riding for their lives. After they scattered and calmed down, well, do I really have to ask which member of your posse first spied the unshod pony tracks leading into the woods, Whitey?"

Jung said, "You must all think I'm really stupid."

Stein said, "Our Lord was betrayed by a follower he trusted, and you'd better not ever say *He* was stupid, hear?"

Longarm told Jung, "You wasn't too dumb to bawl them both out for acting dumb when they kept riding on ahead of the rest of you, pretending to be eager pups and no doubt leading you all farther astray by pretending to see things that wasn't there."

Whitey brightened. "Thunderation! Spud did ride back to tell us him and Slim had been fired on from that cabin they'd spotted up ahead. I gave Slim hell for charging in singlehanded, or saying he had. That was about the time he got mad and quit on me again."

Longarm nodded. "He'd led you far and foolish and he wanted to come back and see if he could figure out where the money they'd been after in the first place might be. When he learned the safe was empty and that I'd been sent up here to offer serious help, he got excited again. He figured I had to be smarter than you, Whitey—no offense—and when I hung around a spell instead of riding off into the dark like I was supposed to, he figured I was on to something and tried to gun me the first time. He never knew I only knew I didn't know nothing and saw no reason to run around in circles."

Kirby horned in to say, "Hold on. If none of them crooks ever headed for Long's Peak in the first place, save as part of the posse, who blew Hamp Hampshire to Kingdom Come after chasing him and Gus Polk off the mountain earlier?"

Longarm looked pained. "I know for a fact Pappy Garson was crazy. He might have been in on the deal. I

172

doubt it. I suspect he just didn't like strangers on his private mountain and, like I said, he'd dead. I found him that way, farther up, after he opened fire on Hamp, Gus, and me."

Stein smiled for the first time since they'd met. "Hot damn! Hamp must have got him, too, as they was shooting it out up there, right?"

Longarm nodded soberly. "That would look nice on paper for the sake of a fellow lawman's record. So, sure, why don't we record it that way? They're both dead, so that's that."

Whitey said, "All right. I see how and why Slim and Spud played me so false. But I'm still confused about that shootout at the smithy this afternoon."

Longarm said, "You were supposed to be. Would I be far wrong in saying you was with Spud McArtle when you heard the gunshots, ran for the smithy, and then Spud said he'd met Slim running in from another direction?"

"Sure. That's about how it happened."

Longarm shook his head. "No, it never. Try it this way. The day of the robbery, as Lefty Page found the noise at least worth passing interest, the smith never turned from his forge as they passed by. He may not have been in on it, but he likely knew about it, and didn't want to have to either lie under oath or bear witness against the father of the girl he was so fond of. With her father's full approval."

Whitey asked, "Then why did Peckerwood Sam get so riled up when he caught June with the smith like that?"

"Like what? Standing together in a neat row, all three of them? All three was shot the same way at close range. It was a pure surprise execution, not the act of an outraged man followed by a running gunfight. Nobody shoots that neat unless they're set steady to fire at stationary targets."

Matt Kincaid groaned. "Talk about stupid! I did find it odd two different men could get off head shots every time. But I still bought the story that murderous young rascal was trying to sell."

Longarm saw that Whitey was still confused. He explained gently, "Everyone, including Slim, knew about the blacksmith and the girl. Slim was one of the few who knew his sidekick, Peckerwood Sam, didn't care. Slim's opinion of the poor drunken degenerate, I mean the father, must have been as low as our own. A desperate drunk who was never paid off for his desperate few moments of sober courage was a loose cannon on the deck to the rest of the gang. A man who'd sell his own daughter for drinking money would hardly be the gent *I'd* trust with a hanging secret. Slim knew Sam knew he'd killed Compten. Whether he demanded anything from Slim or not, Slim knew the older man had a brace of mismatched .38s. After pegging at me with a .36, and failing again, Slim must have felt the sudden need for a change of hardware. He somehow lured or forced Peckerwood Sam to pay a social call on his daughter and her lover. It was likely a friendly visit, from the way they were all standing on the back porch when Slim simply shot the three of them down like dogs, switched guns with one victim, and stepped outside to go through motions only his pal Spud really had to back up. By the time you could work your way back to join them, moving no faster than I would have through a gun-haunted house, they'd had plenty of time to pose the dead more to fit the tale they told you."

Whitey said, "And I *bought* it!"

Longarm said, "That bullet hole in Slim's hat was sort of overdoing it, in my opinion. If we need to prove my own version of what happened, the medical examiners in Boulder will no doubt be proud to dig the slugs out of the two men. If Spud wants to stick to his fool story he's going to have a time convincing any jury of halfway sober men that he saw his pard shoot Peckerwood Sam with a .38 that left a .36 in his head."

Inspector Stein said, "This is all mighty interesting. But who got the *money,* if it wasn't any of the depraved folk you just told us so much about?"

Longarm sighed. "I knew we'd have to get to that sooner or later. Whitey, why don't you stay here and keep Matt company while me and post office take a leak?"

They followed him into the gents' room readily enough, but when Longarm said, "I don't really have to piss. You boys go ahead if you have to," Stein called him a mean thing and insisted, "Where's the damn money? Surely not in *here?*"

Longarm said, "Not hardly. The door's marked 'Gents Only.' Miss Polly Clark has the money. I don't know just where. If I was you I'd wait until she finishes

175

selling out and tries to leave town. She's sure to have it on or about her person then. The rest of the time she fibs just for fun and, if she's hidden it good, you won't *ever* be able to arrest her. I can't, even if I had the goods on her for sure. I hope she didn't have that in mind and that it was just personal admiration, but you never know with women. It's so much easier for them to fake such delicate matters."

The hitherto friendlier Kirby snapped, "Stop boasting about your sex life and tell us what you have on her!"

Longarm said, "You mean what *you* have on her. That was the deal we made. She wasn't in on the robbery. I feared for a time she could be. But I reckon someone hearing a horse was dead might assume, innocent, that you meant it had been shot. Ponies don't just die natural that often."

"Longarm, will you get to the point?"

"The robbery came as a total surprise to her. I'd like you to keep that in mind when you type up a statement for her to sign. She likely will, once you point out it's her first offense and you know she didn't act premeditated."

"How *did* she act, damn it?"

"Greedy, mayhaps a mite desperate. As she sat up sort of confused as the half-ass robbers ran out, she saw they hadn't opened the safe after all. So *she* opened it and hid the money, and who was about to search for it within yards of an open safe when they was mounting up to chase a gang of robbers who more likely had it? That's all there was to it."

"She surely must have known it would cost her her position."

"Sure she did. The paint on her going-out-of-business sign was likely dry before you got around to firing her. What of it? Would you refuse to swap a position paying a petty stipend and a seedy little crossroads store with no paying customers for a safe full of money?"

Stein said, "Yes. But I know some aren't as honest as I was brought up. Can you *prove* any of this?"

Longarm said, "I don't have to. I won't be the arresting officer, thank God. But it's process of elimination. Miss Polly kept insisting she'd locked the safe before the robbery and hadn't opened it for them during. Nobody but her had the combination. There's only two ways to open a good safe like that one: You can crack it open or you can open it proper. It hadn't been cracked, so I knew it had been opened by someone who knew the combination. She said none of her help did. I tried to see if I could figure it out through her bitty window, as, say, a mighty fine safe man might try to. It couldn't be done. Counting the clicks only works when you can see the dial. I couldn't. So any number of clicks from most anywhere meant any old number."

He shook his head sadly and summed it up by saying, "The stupid outlaws couldn't have. Somebody did. She was the only other person in there. It don't add up no other way and I'm sorry as hell. But that money belongs mostly to poor folk."

Kirby nodded. "We'll get it back to one and all, after

we nail her leaving town with it. We can talk about it more down in Boulder, later, after things simmer down."

Longarm frowned. "I wasn't planning on hanging around Boulder, gents."

But Stein said, "You'll have to, at least till the coroner's jury says you can leave."

Chapter 13

Stein had been right. It took the coroner's jury almost three days to decide everyone they could possibly charge with murder was already dead. So it was mid-afternoon when Longarm got back to Denver.

The day was about shot and he hadn't wired he was coming, lest he meet someone interesting aboard the train. But he hadn't. The widow woman up on Sherman Avenue was entertaining house guests from back East and Miss Morgana Floyd of the Arvada Orphan Asylum wasn't speaking to him because she'd found out about the widow woman up on Sherman Avenue. Longarm decided he might as well report in. There wasn't anything to report that he hadn't already told Billy Vail by night letter a couple of days ago, but with any luck he could keep old Billy talking until even he could see it was time to knock off for the day.

When he got there, Henry in the front office said Vail was down the hall jawing with the federal prosecutor. Henry added, "I read your report. I'll be damned if I can figure out how you get Western Union to spell so bad, but I took the liberty of correcting it as I typed it up in triplicate for you to sign."

Longarm smiled down at the clerk. "That was neighborly as hell, Henry. But why are you grinning up at me so smarmy, no offense?"

Henry said, "A lady was just in here looking for you. A real looker. You just missed her, but I know where she's hired a room—for just this weekend, she said."

Longarm frowned. "Well, out with it, Henry, unless you have your own wild-oat plans for this evening, after they cut you loose from that typewriter."

Henry sighed wistfully. "I got the distinct impression she felt sort of wild-oats about you. Some women sure have odd taste in men. She says she's a newspaper gal for the *Kansas City Star*. She's booked in at the Drexal Hotel near the Denver Dry Goods and Department Store."

Longarm laughed. "You got a dirty mind, Henry. But could you do me one more favor?"

Henry looked dubious. "I don't know, Longarm. The last time you got me to lie to the boss you almost got me fired."

Longarm looked innocent. "Heaven forfend, Henry. I wouldn't want you fibbing to Marshal Vail. You don't have to volunteer that I'm back in town yet. But if he twists your arm, it's all right to tell him I went looking for him and might have got lost. He'll likely cool off by Monday morning."

Henry asked, "Who *do* you want me to lie to about you, then?"

Longarm smiled fondly down at him. "You sure have

got to know me since you been working here, old son. You don't have to fib to Miss Wilma Wadsworth unless she comes back looking for me some more. I don't want her to know where I am until it's time for her to head back to K.C."

Henry looked puzzled. "You don't? She's a real looker and sort of flirty-eyed as well. I should think she'd be just what the doctor ordered for a rascal like you."

Longarm looked sheepish. "She sure was. But parting is such sweet sorrow, I don't like to keep at it. Aside from that, I got to thinking aboard the train down from Boulder."

"About women, of course."

"Well, sure. I had a morose *adios* with an even prettier redheaded postmistress just before I left Boulder, Henry. They went and arrested her before I could get out of the county. I didn't have to testify against her and I wasn't about to testify *for* her, but it sort of left me feeling blue about redheaded postmistress gals."

Henry said, "I read your night letter to the boss. He agrees you did right in shoving that can of worms to the Post Office men. What does federal prisoner Polly Clark have to do with Wilma Wadsworth of the *Kansas City Star?*"

Longarm said, "Not a thing, Henry. I ain't feeling nostalgic about female reporters, and even if I was I don't aim to spend a weekend fibbing to *any* reporters about a case we've wrapped up so neat and sort of off-the-record."

He lit a cheroot and asked, "Do you remember telling me a month or so ago about that postmistress out to Aurora getting divorced a week or so earlier?"

Henry nodded. "Sure. I thought you'd be interested in it, since you met up with her that time on that other post office case. What could she possibly have to do with this more recent one?"

Longarm said, "Not a thing, Henry, save for the fact I just remembered she was a redhead, too, and it might cheer me up to talk to a redheaded postmistress who might not be mad as hell at me right now."

Henry laughed despite himself. "If I know you, they'll *both* think you're disgusting in the near future."

Watch for

LONGARM AND THE COTTONWOOD CURSE

one hundred and first novel in the bold
LONGARM series from Jove

coming in May!

ENTER TO WIN A
FABULOUS WESTERN VACATION!

#100 WESTERN JUBILEE SWEEPSTAKES
OFFICIAL ENTRY FORM

To enter the sweepstakes, please fill in the information below and return it to:

**#100 WESTERN JUBILEE Sweepstakes
The Berkley Publishing Group, Dept. SE
200 Madison Avenue, New York, NY 10016**

No purchase necessary. Void where prohibited by law. For complete rules, see below.

Name _____

Address _____

City/State _____ Zip _____

Phone _____

Mail this entry form no later than May 31, 1987. A facsimile may be used in lieu of official entry form.

- -

FIRST PRIZE: Winner will receive a round-trip airticket for two persons plus a 5 day stay at a luxury western ranch (not including personal expenses i.e. liquor, laundry, etc.). No purchase necessary.

- -

1. On an official entry form or a plain 3" x 5" piece of paper, hand print your name, address and telephone number and mail your entry in a hand-addressed envelope (#10) to #100 WESTERN JUBILEE SWEEPSTAKES, Berkley Publishing Group, 200 Madison Avenue, New York, NY 10016. No mechanical reproduction of entries permitted.

2. Entries must be postmarked no later than May 31, 1987. Not responsible for misdirected or lost mail.

3. Enter as often as you wish but each entry must be mailed separately. The winner will be determined on June 15th, 1987 in a random drawing from among all entries. The winner will be notified by mail.

4. This sweepstake is open to all U.S. residents 18 years of age or older. Void where prohibited by law. Employees of MCA and their families, their retailers and distributors, their respective advertising, promotion and production agencies are not eligible.

5. Taxes on all prizes are the sole responsibility of the prize winner who may be required to sign and return a statement of eligibility within 14 days of notification. Names and likenesses of winners may be used for promotion purposes.

6. Travel and accommodation (based on double-occupancy) are subject to space and departure availability. All travel must be completed by December 15, 1987. No substitution of prizes is permitted.

7. For a list of prizewinners send a self-addressed stamped envelope to: #100 WESTERN JUBILEE PRIZEWINNERS
The Berkley Publishing Group, Dept. LG 200 Madison Avenue, New York, NY 10016